The Gift
of
Charms

The Land of
Dragor

The Gift
of
Charms

JULIA SUZUKI

JOHN BLAKE

Published by John Blake Publishing Ltd,
3 Bramber Court, 2 Bramber Road,
London W14 9PB, England

www.johnblakepublishing.co.uk

www.facebook.com/johnblakebooks 🖪
twitter.com/jblakebooks 🖪

First published in paperback in 2014.
Private edition originally published in hardback,
as *Yoshiko and the Gift of Charms*, in 2011.

ISBN: 978-1-78219-924-3

British Library Cataloguing-in-Publication Data:
a catalogue record for this book is available from the British Library.

Design by www.envydesign.co.uk

Printed in Great Britain by CPI Group (UK) Ltd

3 5 7 9 10 8 6 4 2

Papers used by John Blake Publishing are natural, recyclable products made from
wood grown in sustainable forests. The manufacturing processes conform to the
environmental regulations of the country of origin.

www.landofdragor.com
Visit Guya's mystical cave where he will reveal
to you your own magical charm.

To those who believed –
you gave me the wings.

Contents

Epigraph

'Many great creatures first roamed the earth with us,' Ma'am Sancy announced to her class, her wings held wide. 'There were all different types. Some had trunks and tusks as long as their bodies. Others had claws that enabled them to leap through the highest trees in the forests.' The younglings all gazed at their history teacher, as her words captured their full attention.

'At first they were happy to share the lands with us. But as the years went by, the earth moved and the seas divided,' she continued. 'Some of the dinosaurs sought survival by breeding with our dragon ancestors creating a super-evil species known as dragsaurs – monsters who were willing do anything to take over the world and destroy us!' One of the orange Mida dragons gasped in horror at the thought of such beasts.

'But despite their efforts, and indeed after many great wars, both dragsaurs and dinosaurs became extinct. It was only us dragons who managed to survive the new climates, though we became slaves to man. That is until one great rebellion, when after receiving a special gift we managed to escape and flee to the Land of Dragor, where we now remain hidden below the smoky mists.'

Prologue

The Strange Egg

First came the whispers, then the rumours, and by New Birth's Eve every dragon was gossiping that Kiara had laid a strange egg.

Some said it was square, like the toffee-nuts gathered by the sweet-toothed Bushki dragons. Whilst other dragons claimed they had heard a strange sound from Kiara and Ketu's cave as they had flown overhead, as if the egg was singing. And the older dragons said it was the grey colour of a sickly hatchling, that when the shell broke the Hudrah dragon would arrive with her black wicker basket to ferry the infant away.

Each clan had its own Hudrah, who would watch over the births. But as the night darkened on Kiara's cave there was no sign of her coming.

Then a great crack echoed around the mountain.

The egg was hatching.

Kiara had not left the nest for three seasons. She had sat patiently in the same position day and night, feeding on mouthfuls of powdery quartz whilst hiding her egg from prying eyes. Now she looked on with Ketu by her side as the shell opened.

It split into two, then four, and a determined little pink snout became visible.

Suddenly, a dark shape appeared at the mouth of the cave – Yula, the Nephan clan Hudrah, had arrived.

Some said Hudrahs possessed the sharpest of hearing that could sense the first pecks inside an eggshell from far distances, whilst others thought it was the black stones they wore around their necks that had magical powers to foretell a new birth.

But on this occasion the Hudrah's powers to predict a birth had not worked soon enough. Yula rushed through the cave entrance, her large red body and silver cape barely squeezing through.

'Oh horror!' she exclaimed. 'It has cracked open already!'

Healthy dragon eggs were a delicate lilac colour, and after birth lay in pretty pieces around the baby-pink hatchling, which within hours would change into one of the seven dragon clan colours.

This eggshell was very different. It was every colour of the rainbow and jewelled like the contents of a treasure chest. It swirled with yellow, green, blue and violet and shone and sparkled in the firelight.

The pieces of the shell fell away.

Kiara breathed out in relief to see that her hatchling was the same pink as all others. The tiny dragon wiggled to dislodge the last piece of shell.

Kiara moved to help nudge it off with her nose, but Yula stopped her.

'Let me see the hatchling make his own way,' she insisted.

The determined little dragon shook off the last piece of shell and Kiara immediately scooped him up in great delight and nuzzled him.

'Oh, isn't he perfect?' she exclaimed, holding him out to the others. 'See his straight little muzzle, his lovely ears and just look at his big green eyes!'

Ketu looked at the newborn, full of pride. 'Our beautiful son,' he said, watching Kiara holding him aloft and then bringing the baby close back against her chest.

Kiara continued to smile. 'Yoshiko,' she said. 'His name shall be Yoshiko,' and with that she leaned forward to kiss her hatchling.

Then there was a flash of black.

For the first time in her history as a Hudrah, Yula had taken out the black wicker basket. Ketu moved quickly to protect Kiara and the baby hatchling.

'What do you mean by this, Yula?' Kiara exclaimed. 'Our hatchling is a perfectly healthy addition to the Nephan clan!'

Yula shook her head slowly. 'Step aside, both of you,' she snarled. 'Do not obstruct the Hudrah in her work. This hatchling is cursed. It is my duty to protect the clans of our land so I must take him away immediately!'

Kiara stared at Yula defiantly. 'There is nothing wrong with my hatchling,' she said. 'Any who look at him would know he is a blessed creature. There is no need for him to be . . .' But she could not even bring herself to say the words.

'The black wicker basket is for the good of all,' insisted Yula boldly. 'Give me your son, or I shall use my Hudrah powers to take him from you. Once the basket has emerged there is no hope for this dragon.'

Ketu stepped forward quickly to intervene, taking

Yula calmly by the shoulder. 'It has been too long a night for you, ma'am,' he said. 'Thirteen births so far and this your fourteenth.'

Yula nodded with uncertainty.

'Our dragon is as normal as any young hatchling, who all come in different shapes and sizes!' continued Ketu. 'As for the shell, please look again. It is only the reflection of the flames that makes it glint strangely. Besides,' he added, 'you must be tired and I have not yet paid you for your services.'

Taking out a purse he counted out twenty glass stones and pressed them into Yula's hand.

The old dragon's claws held open as she looked down in wonder at the generous offering. It was ten times more than she had expected to be paid for the whole night. Her breath slowed as she carefully reconsidered the situation before finally replying.

'True enough, Ketu, there is nothing physically wrong with your dragon.'

One by one her yellowed talons closed around the stones.

Ketu breathed a sigh of relief as Yula slid the black wicker basket away under her cape and pulled out instead the large birthing book. She turned to a new page.

'Name of hatchling?' she asked, holding a thick charcoal pen in her claw.

'Yoshiko,' Ketu replied.

'Distinguishing features?'

'None,' said Ketu firmly.

Yula carefully recorded the details of the newborn into her book. 'He will be either a curse or a blessing,' she murmured, looking to where Yoshiko's tiny snout was sniffing the warm air of the cave. But Kiara wasn't listening. She was far too busy stroking his tiny scales in delight.

'Yoshiko,' said Kiara as Yula stood to leave. 'Yoshiko.'

1

Fire School

As seasons passed, the talk about the egg and Yoshiko's birth faded amongst the clans. Yoshiko was now the vibrant red colour of his clan, but in the daylight Kiara noticed something different. His scales would sometimes take on a different tone. Like a hint of pink, or a violet haze, but the change would be so tiny that no other dragon paid attention. New Birth's Eve turned to Green Earth Night, Red Seventh Moon became Yellow Harvest, and before Kiara and Ketu knew it Yoshiko had weathered ten winters.

* * *

Yoshiko was up and pestering his elders hours before school was due to start, and eventually it was a tired Ketu who dropped down from his perch to calm his excitable son.

'I don't feel like any breakfast!' announced Yoshiko. But Ketu had already drawn out the heavy pan and was filling it with salt-rock and herbs. He blew a little spurt of fire into the mixture and stirred in some dark peat.

'First day at Fire School and you will need the maximum energy to make flames,' he announced, heaping ladles of the porridge into a large wooden bowl and placing it on the stone table where the family ate their meals.

Kiara flopped down from her perch and Yoshiko eyed her hopefully.

'Your elder is right,' she agreed as she handed him a wire net. 'And, here, you'll need this for today.'

Yoshiko took it gladly. He'd seen other young dragons using the copper nets to carry their equipment to school and envied the casual way in which they hooked them over their wings to hold items securely whilst in flight.

'It has your midday meal in it and lots of snacks, plus all the other equipment you will need,' explained Kiara.

She stuck her snout into the net and retrieved a heavy glass jar in her teeth.

'You will need to put this whale-fruit on,' she added, nudging the pot towards him. 'Make sure you cover yourself completely, and don't forget your ears.'

Yoshiko opened the jar and grimaced at the smell of the jelly substance.

Kiara snatched it up and began smearing it thickly on his chest as Yoshiko pulled away. 'Be still! Be still!' she insisted. 'It will stop you getting scale-ache from the intense heat of the Fire Pit. You will need it until your scales harden up. Be sure to smear it on again after you've eaten at midday.'

The whale-fruit hadn't dimmed Yoshiko's mood as he eagerly hooked the wire school-net through his wing. He and all the other younglings of his age could fly short distances but none of them were quite ready to journey the distance of the land. Yoshiko climbed on to his elder's back, ready to take the journey to the far side of Dragor.

Ketu took off gracefully as Kiara waved from the cave entrance. Yoshiko stared down in wonder as they swept across the sky. He gazed down at the steaming mud pools next to the Fire Which Must Never Go Out and then across the Great Waters to the view of the tallest of all their mountains.

The dragons banked east, and Yoshiko looked across curiously. 'Why are we flying this way?' he asked. 'It looks quickest to fly west over the mountains.'

'Well spotted, Yoshiko,' replied Ketu. 'However, if we flew that way we would pass over Cattlewick Cave and we are all forbidden to do so.'

'What's Cattlewick Cave?' asked Yoshiko.

'It is a very mysterious cave that no one knows much about,' replied Ketu. 'An old dragon called Guya has lived alone there for many years and Kinga our great leader ordered that no dragon should disturb him. We must keep away from his mountain.'

Yoshiko tried to imagine why any dragon would want to live in complete seclusion as Ketu flew east over the flowery Mida meadows. They swept through a cloud of blue butterflies that were hovering over the grassy hills and then fell into the thick flock of elders also taking their younglings for their first day at Fire School.

*   *   *

A huge dragon was on his haunches with his wings wide in welcome as the dragons came to land at the foot of

Dragor's largest mountain. His scales were a deep rusty red and were raised into thick leathery ridges.

'That's the head of Fire School, his name is Ayo,' said Ketu. 'He is also head of the elite Guard Dragon.'

Yoshiko looked on in awe.

'The Guard Dragon train in special fire pits,' Ketu continued. 'Their scales are so thick that it would be hard for a spear to pierce them and they can resist most flames.'

Yoshiko's eyes dropped to his own skin, which was still so soft that the scales were barely visible.

'When can younglings like me walk into the Fire Pit?' he asked Ketu.

'No particular time, whenever you are ready,' said his elder. 'At first, even standing at the hot stone-wall entrance will be unbearable. But you will soon adjust to the heat. After a few weeks you shouldn't need the whale-fruit for protection,' he continued, 'and after a season you should be able to brave the walk through the outside of the Pit, although most dragons never get good enough to walk right into the centre.

'Anyway,' he added. 'Before then you must learn to blow fire and to fly properly.'

* * *

Yoshiko soaked up the image that was in front of him. The depths of the school Fire Pit was glowing the brightest shade of orange and the sides were stacked high with rocks to prevent any fire escaping. Behind it stood the Fire School cave entrance and two large torches burned on each side. To the right of this a large stack of rocks had been constructed to make a crescent-shaped wall. Metal targets of various sizes had been built into it. Dragons who had reached seventeen winters were aiming at these silver pennant-shapes, belching out mighty columns of flame that struck in a dizzying flash of light.

Behind the Fire Pit was the largest cave Yoshiko had ever seen. It looked like it had taken a hundred moons to carve out and from his position near the entrance he could see inside that many dark paths led from it deeply into the mountain.

Outside the entrance was a mighty stone tablet, on which were etched the words:

THE COMMANDMENTS OF GOADAH.

Yoshiko read the notice.

1. ALWAYS KEEP ALIGHT THE FIRE WHICH MUST NEVER GO OUT

This great fire must be kept smoking at all times to keep the Land of Dragor hidden. It is the honorary role of the Guard Dragons to keep the fire burning day and night.

2. NEVER LEAVE DRAGOR

No dragon must ever leave Dragor. To do so is to put all the clans in danger of being discovered again by humans who will destroy all dragons.

3. NEVER FLY ABOVE SURION MOUNTAIN

Here stands the tallest mountain in Dragor, named after the dragon hero Surion. It serves as a marker that no dragon is ever to fly above.

4. RESPECT THE LEADER

Honour the leader of Dragor and obey his rules at all times.

'Reading up on your Commandments, I see!' Ketu commented as he looked over Yoshiko's shoulder. 'These rules were made when dragons first came to live in Dragor and we consider them sacred!'

'What happens if the Commandments are broken?' asked Yoshiko.

'Any dragon who does not obey the four rules has to go to our prison,' replied Ketu. 'It is a dark and damp cave that no dragon can tunnel his way out of, and it has the thickest gate made of iron.'

2

Making Flames

Another elder dragon landed next to them with a young, particularly small female dragon called Amlie. She hopped down from his back carrying an identical net to Yoshiko's. They touched wings, and both broke into wide smiles.

Amlie and Yoshiko both lived in Nephan territory in neighbouring caves, and as hatchlings had regularly played in their nearby mountains.

'I didn't think you would be starting at Fire School yet!' said Yoshiko warmly. 'I thought your elders weren't going to let you start until next season.'

'I wanted to be in the same class as you,' she stuttered in her high-pitched, hasty tone. 'I practised and practised to make a grown-up flame to convince them I was big enough to come, and look!'

She swelled her small chest to an impossible size, screwing up her face in the process and gasped out a rush of air that smelled like paraffin. But no fire accompanied it.

'Wait,' she said, inflating herself again. This time the exhalation was met with a little shower of sparks, and a flame, no more than a talon-width across, hung off her bottom lip.

'That's a good start,' Yoshiko remarked.

'Oh, I can do way better than that,' continued Amlie. 'I sometimes get the timing wrong like that. When I am matching the air and the spark I sometimes click too early, but my elder says if I keep up my good progress then I'll soon be spurting really long jets of flame.'

A sudden sound drew everyone's attention; an enormous fireball signalled that it was time for school to begin.

'All the younglings up to the crescent!' Ayo announced in a bellowing tone. 'Any elders who wish to stay and watch over their younglings for the first hour may all assemble behind, at the observation deck.'

Amlie and Yoshiko exchanged glances then followed Ayo's instruction.

Just as the younglings and elders divided, a purple dragon landed with a loud thud. He was clearly far later than any of the other arrivals, but still didn't seem in any rush. He unfurled his large wing casually and let his youngling hop down. The elder had a shifty appearance. His son was large for his age with brown horns protruding over his dark eyes and a look that suggested he already hated Fire School and everyone in it.

A queue was forming. The younglings were being organised into a long line by two Guard Dragons with Ayo watching over them all.

'Ah, you must be Igorr,' he remarked as the new arrival stomped over. 'Take your place over there.' He pointed to the back of the queue where the younglings were huddled together. Amlie nodded at Igorr as he moved behind her, but in return he just stared back meanly.

'My elders say I should mix only with Alanas of my own breed,' he snarled whilst looking around busily to where some other purple dragons were huddled. 'You red Nephan dragons think you know it all!'

'And you Alanas are always telling lies and causing bad business,' shot back Amlie, glaring defiantly at Igorr.

Igorr narrowed his eyes even more at Yoshiko who stood next in line. 'Well, well, well! Look who it is!' he exclaimed. 'My elder told me all about you. You are Yoshiko. Yoshiko – the weirdo. The one who came from the strange egg that the Hudrah should have taken away in her black wicker basket.'

The colour left Yoshiko's face as he took in Igorr's words. 'What are you talking about?'

Igorr was about to reply, but before he could make a retort the attention of all the younglings was drawn back to Ayo as he beat his wings together, causing the great torches to flare.

'Welcome to Fire School!' he announced.

'All younglings will now be having lessons in how to breathe fire,' Ayo went on. 'But we must all take great heed, for fire can also destroy as much as it helps create. Misuse of your talent could burn down the forests, dragons can be badly injured or even killed. My job is to ensure that you younglings know how to use your fire properly.' He gazed up and down the rows of dragons eyeing them intently, then continued. 'Now, I know that many of you younglings have come here today excited at the prospect of making a flame or two, so as a special treat for today I shall allow you to do a little target play. But first, you must learn the basic theories from me. Now, take out your wooden boards and charcoal sticks.'

Yoshiko took out the equipment from his bag and as he did so he glanced over to Igorr. He noticed that the purple dragon's muzzle was twisted in confusion and that he was looking about him anxiously.

'Have you not brought anything with you?' said Amlie as she also noticed that Igorr didn't have a net of his own.

'How was I supposed to know?' grumbled Igorr, looking distraught. All the other pupils had their wooden boards poised expectantly. 'No one told me I needed to bring . . . whatever that is,' and he gestured with uncertainty to the stick of charcoal.

'Here, you can share mine,' said Yoshiko, moving the board between them. Igorr looked up reluctantly, and then Ayo began to speak again.

'This morning I will be covering the basics of fire-making, that being dragon-anatomy, fire-sense, fire-theory and the history of Surion. The more you pay attention the quicker we will get to the fun things.'

He pointed the edge of his wing meaningfully around the circle of younglings. 'Until I have finished I don't want to see any of you practising. Do you understand? Until I say you can make fire, no dragon makes fire.'

'What is the point of learning all this totally boring stuff if I can already breathe fire?' Igorr muttered. 'I can hit a target from twelve paces – this is all a complete waste of my time!'

Ayo looked at Igorr sternly to silence him.

'What is the most important part of fire-breathing?' Ayo asked, staring around the whole group of younglings for an answer.

'The fire-gases!' a young voice shouted out.

Ayo peered to where an orange dragon was sitting. 'Good answer,' he said. 'That's a very important part of making fire, and for those of you who don't know, there are fire-gases being made in all your bellies as we speak.'

He gestured to his stomach. 'When a dragon enters his tenth winter his abdomen changes,' he explained. 'Two chambers are formed which create two different liquids. When these are mixed together they blend into a special flammable gas. Who can tell me what flammable means?'

Another dragon spoke out. 'It means you can set it on fire,' she said.

'Correct,' said Ayo. 'So, all of you have these pits in

your stomach as we speak. That's why you'll have gone through metamorphosis.

'Do you remember? When your stomach started to make noises of its own accord and you developed an embarrassing tendency to burp in public?'

The younglings giggled. Most had gone through Metamorphosis with its commonly known side effects a few seasons ago but as if in response to Ayo a small blue dragon's stomach growled noisily, followed by a really loud burp. The younglings near where he sat roared with laughter.

'The second part of fire-making,' continued Ayo. 'The dragon tongue is vital in making flames.'

He clicked his own tongue and a few sparks shot forth.

'See these ridges here,' he pointed to the drawing on his own board as he held it up. 'The technical name for these is carbon-teeth.' Several pupils scribbled this down and he pointed to the shape of the ridges, which were curved slightly like tiny claws.

'These curved shapes are one half of what makes the sparks that ignite the flame,' said Ayo. 'Every dragon is born with these. Even tiny hatchlings have the little diamond-protrusions on their tongues,' he paused.

'And there is another important part of making fire.' This time Ayo tapped the top of his mouth with a claw.

'The flint bones,' he said, 'which harden around the top of the mouth and when they are properly set the tongue can be used to strike against them and make sparks.'

He drew a mouth around the tongue on the board and tapped at it. 'The basic technique is very simple,' he said, 'although it does not usually come naturally and has to be taught. Can anyone tell me a dragon for whom this method was a natural skill?'

Now all the younglings flung their wings up, jostling to be chosen. Ayo pointed out an orange dragon.

'Surion!' he announced proudly.

'That's right,' said Ayo. 'And what was unusual about Surion?'

'His egg,' said Igorr loudly, glaring at Yoshiko. 'Surion was a cursed dragon. He came from a strange-coloured egg!'

Ayo shook his head. 'Not many dragons think Surion was a curse, Igorr. Almost all in our land praise him as a great dragon and our hero. Do you all know much about the legend of Surion?' he asked, addressing the younglings before him.

Most of the dragons nodded their heads but some looked at him blankly, so Ayo continued.

'Surion is the most famous dragon in all our history because he was the first dragon to make flames. No creature before Surion could breathe fire. He taught other dragons to use fire to escape from being the slaves of humans. It enabled us to win our freedom. There was a mighty battle that we today know as the Battle of Surion, and since then all of us dragons have lived in our own secret land where no humans can find us. The Commandments of Goadah keep us safe and secret from capture.' All the dragons were listening attentively except Igorr who was fidgeting impatiently.

'As the lessons progress you will learn that the dragon's fire is our greatest accomplishment. Each different dragon clan uses their fire for many different purposes. Some dragons make exquisite metalwork, others the most beautiful pots from the red clay of our hills.' He waved his wings expansively. 'Today I am not going to get into any further argument as to whether Surion from the red egg brought dragons freedom or cursed us to live in hiding,' he said. 'That is for your history teacher to debate with you. Our Council has enough challenges to deal with, doing all they can to protect us from external threats. It is important that we are united, talented and strong. In Fire School I need you all to get along.' He looked out at them as if daring anyone to disagree.

'So now I imagine all of you will want to make the biggest flames that you possibly can,' he said.

The younglings nodded enthusiastically.

'Well then,' said Ayo. 'Time to give it a try.' He unfolded his wings to gesture them to move towards the fire targets.

The younglings set their nets down to the floor and trooped closer to the crescent.

Their elders were now directly above them watching from the viewing deck.

Igorr's face lit up suddenly.

'There is my elder, Gandar!' he cried, grabbing Yoshiko's wing in his excitement. 'Do you see him? Do you see him?' Igorr started waving frantically.

Yoshiko looked up into the viewing deck to see two large, grey, hooded eyes staring down at them.

The older Alana nodded his snout slightly, but didn't return his son's wave. Then he looked up at the sun, as if calculating how much more time he would need to spend at the school.

'Line up in groups of five in front of the targets!' said

Ayo. 'Anyone who would like to give their turn a miss today please wait at the side over there and watch how the other younglings try.'

Around a dozen yellow and orange dragons began to shuffle away over to the other side of the crescent and several of them looked very relieved.

The first younglings then took their position in front of the targets and at Ayo's command around half managed to produce a full flame that left their bodies, whilst the others made little jets of fire or sparks. None hit a target.

Yoshiko watched with uncertainty, and then looked back to Amlie who was almost bursting with impatience to start.

He watched Amlie step forward ready for her attempt. Igorr was busy warming himself up by strutting around and puffing out his chest whilst making loud grunts.

Amlie stood directly in front of the target. She puffed her chest in and out three times and then unleashed a football-sized flame that fell within a few feet of the target. Applause fell from the observation deck.

Yoshiko looked carefully down the line as the next younglings prepared to take aim. Igorr was next to step up, and was eyeing the target with an assured look. He balled up his chest, narrowed his eyes, and as Ayo gave the word let out an impressive column of flame which came close enough to nudge the edge of his target.

Ayo beat his wings in applause, and Igorr looked overjoyed as he turned to look up to the viewing deck to see his elder's reaction. The happiness dropped suddenly from him, and his wings collapsed despondently against his body.

Yoshiko turned to see that Igorr's elder was no longer watching from the viewing deck and had not stayed to see his son's fire at all.

Igorr stalked past the row of younglings, and as he did Yoshiko put out a friendly wing. 'Why is your elder not here?' he asked.

Igorr turned on him furiously.

'Why is my elder not here?' he spat. 'Why should anyone's elder be here? I'm not a baby like you. I don't need my elder looking on.' He marched off towards some other purple dragons, and as he joined them he turned his full attention back to glare at Yoshiko.

Feeling even more disconcerted by the angry gaze, Yoshiko stepped forward to the mark, and on Ayo's command he puffed up his chest as much as he could. Keeping the target in sight, he raised his tongue to the back of his mouth, and as the command came made a loud whooshing sound. A stream of air flew from his belly, and he clicked his tongue as fast as he could. But nothing came out and he dropped his snout in embarrassment. A cry came suddenly from the sidelines.

'Did you see that? Yoshiko tried to hit the target but he cannot even make a spark!'

Yoshiko looked to the side to see that the jibe had come from Igorr, who was looking jubilant now and was nudging his new friends to enjoy the joke.

'What is the point of having your elder here if you can't even make a flame for him?' Igorr continued. 'What a waste of time it's been for him.'

Amlie came and stood by Yoshiko and that fuelled Igorr even more.

'You are stupid, stupid in every way! Even your name. Yoshiko sounds like a girl's name to me – probably because of those silly eyelashes and sissy green eyes that you have. And even your titchy girlfriend can make better fire than you! We shall have to call you Feddy from now on, after the dragon who couldn't make flames!'

Feddy was a storybook dragon considered useless because he was unable to breathe fire. He was instead appointed the job of collecting rubbish in the marketplace where flames weren't needed. It was a popular story amongst young dragons, but no one wanted to be like Feddy.

Yoshiko felt his scales turning darker in his embarrassment. 'My mother told me she called me Yoshiko because she thinks it sounds powerful,' he replied.

'Powerful, ha-ha-ha!' Igorr cackled. 'Yeah, about as powerful as your puff!' The other Alanas roared with laughter at Igorr's joke, their loud sniggers could be heard across Fire School and Yoshiko hung his head in shame.

'Other younglings can't make fire!' Amlie shouted. 'At least Yoshiko was brave enough to try!' But her small voice could barely be heard over the Alanas.

Igorr turned his head to her mockingly.

'My name for him is Feddy from now on.' And there was something so nasty in his look that his group nodded in agreement rather than contradict him.

The hours ahead that day brought nothing but heartache to Yoshiko. He did his best to ignore the taunts from Igorr and the other Alana dragons during the midday meal but by the afternoon all the purple dragons were calling him Feddy. As they trooped into the final class of the day Yoshiko realised that he had around him an entire gang of enemies.

3

The Ageless Ones

Flares were released to signal the end of school and Ketu was already outside the Fire School entrance. He noticed Yoshiko's sad face as he walked over to greet him.

'I saw you today at the targets,' he said. 'You did really well going up there.'

Yoshiko shook his head angrily. 'It was a disaster. I should have stayed at home with the hatchlings who can't make fire.'

'Yoshiko, when I was at Fire School it wasn't any different,' Ketu replied. 'Some dragons were very cruel then too. But I know now why they act this way!'

Yoshiko looked intrigued. 'Why?' he asked.

'They do it as they don't want anyone noticing what they are bad at,' he said. 'They do it to take the attention off the important things that they can't do.'

Yoshiko looked unconvinced. 'It's called Fire School for a reason,' he said. 'Making fire is what we are there to do.'

'Think about the different clans in our land,' replied Ketu. 'How many dragons spend all their days making fire?'

'All dragons do,' said Yoshiko. 'Some use it to make books and papers. Others use it to make explosions when they build caves.'

Ketu shook his head. 'Not quite. Fire is only used for some of the most elaborate paperwork,' he said. 'A lot of the time dragons use charcoal sticks to write as it is quicker that way. And the dragons making our caves mainly use their horns. If they couldn't make explosions with their fire in certain sections it would take them longer, but they could still make beautiful caves.'

Yoshiko frowned. 'But the best dragons, the Guard Dragons, they use fire most of all.'

'The Guards are trained so they don't have to use fire,' replied Ketu. 'The very best Guards train only for necessity should they fall under threat.' He lowered himself so that Yoshiko could jump on board.

'Come, let's go.'

Yoshiko nodded. 'I just wanted you to see me make fire like the others did,' he added with a sigh as he hopped on to his father's back.

Ketu took to the air and flew straight over the Great Waters.

'Where are we going?' said Yoshiko. 'It's the other way home.'

'To the marketplace. I have something to pick up.'

Yoshiko looked down as Ketu drew nearer to the flowery fields of the Mida clan, and finally settled in a large market square.

Dragons of all different colours were walking about.

Yoshiko's eyes settled on two identical dragons. They appeared to be waiting for something and stood apart from all the others.

'Who are they?' asked Yoshiko, pointing towards them as he slid off Ketu's back.

The two dragonesses were the deep indigo blue of the Saiga clan, but had the most unusual faces that were almost perfectly smooth and expressionless with dull, colourless eyes. Hanging on chains around their necks were two large white stones.

'Those are the Ageless Ones,' said Ketu, nodding respectfully towards them. 'The twin dragons of the Saiga clan.'

Yoshiko had heard of the twins. They were often talked about with mystery by other young dragons.

Nothing of their pasts was known, not even their age, which was why they were known as the Ageless Ones. Even more mysterious than this, any attempt to communicate with them was met either with silence, or by a strange sound uttered in duet. Certain questions, or the right time of year, could prompt them to take a deep breath in tandem, and then huff out a steady stream of '*Yeeaa*'.

It was the only sound they made, and most dragons thought the Ageless Ones were simply witless.

'Those stones around their necks are opals!' Ketu inclined his head, but didn't point. Yoshiko looked at the light-coloured gems. They seemed to swirl with mystical colours and patterns. 'The Hudrah swear that the stones give out a magical energy,' said Ketu, 'and the Hudrahs, they know about such things.'

It was the first time Yoshiko had heard Ketu mention the Hudrah of his own accord.

Now that he was older he'd started to notice that both his elders steered the conversation to different topics when he tried to ask about the Nephan clan Hudrah.

Yoshiko had seen black stones swinging from the necks of the Hudrahs when they were in the air.

'Wait here,' said Ketu. 'I have to buy some fish from the market traders; they will bargain harder if they see I have a youngling with me.'

Yoshiko nodded, and watched Ketu retreat towards the fishing stalls. It was the first time he had been left alone away from his own mountain area, and the view was fascinating.

The chatter of the dragons as they traded with each other made a hum and in the far corners he could make out the smoking mud pools where some of the older dragons basked. It was beginning to grow darker now and Yoshiko glanced up.

Kiara had once told him that far up above hung balls of flaming gas that lit the night sky. But these sky-fires were too small to be seen through the smoky mists that rose from mud pools and the smoke from the Fire Which Must Never Go Out.

Yoshiko stood wondering what it might be like to fly from Dragor and see such sights but dismissed the thought guiltily, remembering that all dragons must obey the Commandments of Goadah.

A strange noise brought him back to reality.

'*Yeeeaa.*'

Yoshiko was startled, and looked around.

Suddenly he realised where the sound was coming from.

It was the Ageless Ones. They were looking straight at him.

Cautiously, Yoshiko walked towards them. No other dragons were nearby, and he turned his head to see Ketu in the distance haggling over a glittering fish.

'*Yeeaa.*' The sound came again.

Slowly Yoshiko drew close to them, staring into the bottomless eyes of the twin dragons.

'Can you . . . can you hear me?' He asked them. But his question was met with silence.

He stood for a moment, wondering what went on behind their empty eyes. Then, as he watched, the two dragons slowly raised their arms in unison, and rested a single talon on the stones around each of their necks.

Yoshiko felt the world around him turn to warm

treacle. The marketplace faded and he felt himself pulled along with the swirling colours of their white stones.

In front of him the faces of the two dragons merged into one face, which seemed to contain in it the wisdom of many ages, their eyes had begun to sparkle. Then the mouth opened and began to speak.

'Dragor's destiny.'

Yoshiko took a step back, and as he did so the warmth of the strange new world faded and the bright colours of the marketplace returned.

He blinked for a moment as the clamour of dragons buying and selling crashed back into his ears.

In front of him the two indigo dragons were staring back placidly as if nothing had happened.

Had he imagined it all?

Then Yoshiko felt something hot clasped in his claws. Mystified, he brought his wing up to his face and slowly uncurled the talons. Inside was a smooth round stone. It was clear like the glass stones used by dragons to pay for items. But in its depths were sparkles of turquoise, gold and pink.

'Ready to go?' Ketu was by his side, clutching a parcel of fish.

Yoshiko tucked the gemstone behind one of his scales under his wing.

He clambered silently on to Ketu's back, wondering whether he should tell his elder what strange thing had just occurred.

But Ketu seemed anxious and distracted. He began flapping in preparation to take off much more quickly than usual.

As they flew up into the sky Yoshiko caught a pair of narrow eyes staring up at them from the marketplace.

Yoshiko pointed down. 'Yula the Nephan Hudrah is staring at us,' he said.

'Oh, I am sure she is not looking at us in particular,' replied Ketu, a little too quickly.

But as they made their distance Yoshiko could still feel the Hudrah's glare.

* * *

They landed back in Nephan territory and Yoshiko sneaked another quick look at the gemstone. As he held it out, he saw that the colours inside had stopped flashing. It was as if it had lost its magic. He hid it away again under his wing, wondering what to make of it.

4

Home Sweet Home

That afternoon Kiara had picked her favourite blossoms from the Nephan woods to fill the cave. A dozen pink and orange fireflowers now sat in a wooden vase at the hearth of the fire. Considered almost sacred, fireflowers were so named as the buds only opened to the flames of the dragon cave fires, scenting the homes with the sweetest welcoming aroma. She had also made a limestone pie and was taking it from the embers of the fire when they returned home. Yoshiko immediately sniffed the delicious wafts of dinner and the sight of the beautiful cave brightened his spirit. He rushed over to the stove where a large cauldron of stew was cooking.

'When can we eat?' he said, giving Kiara a nuzzle.

'Not too long from now,' she said. 'Why don't you go and do some fire-breathing practice and I'll call you when it's ready.'

Yoshiko went to the back of the cave where Ketu had set up a special area for him. A metal pennant-shaped fire target was positioned at Yoshiko's height against the back wall. It was the largest size – for beginners – the type crafted especially for younglings just starting at Fire School, and the initial 'Y' had been specially engraved on it. Yoshiko looked at it excitedly.

He began sucking in air noisily as Ketu came to help Kiara ease the pie from the coals.

'Did he do well in school?' asked Kiara, anxiously.

Ketu nodded. 'He joined the practice ranks when other dragons who couldn't make fire sat it out, and he tried even though he couldn't do it. He coped even when some dragons laughed at him.'

Kiara's face dropped. 'Other dragons laughed at him?'

'He had the strength of character to get up and try. With that kind of bravery a few sniggers shouldn't bother him.'

'Who were the dragons laughing at him?' she asked horrified.

'Who do you think?' said Ketu. 'Gandar's youngling Igorr was at the bottom of it. He can already make good fire. I imagine he's learned at the expense of more important lessons.'

Kiara scoffed. 'He'll end up getting too full of himself with his fire-making and get thrown out of the Guard Dragons, just like his elder was for nearly burning down the Nephan forest.'

Ketu raised a talon as a caution for her to keep her voice down. 'No one is supposed to know why Gandar was asked to leave the Guard Dragons, Kiara. If Yoshiko finds out it could be all over the school, and we don't want to be known as the rumour spreaders. Leave that to the Alana clan.'

Kiara lowered her head in response, but she still looked angry.

From the other side of the cave Yoshiko sensed his elders were talking about him and his day.

It provoked a strong feeling to boil inside him as he remembered Igorr's taunts again.

A burning sensation seemed to grow within him, and he tried to catch hold of it as he stared at the target. It was as if a picture of fire was in front of him and he felt his scales tingle all over in a strange rush.

Yoshiko turned towards the rock face. He was breathing deeply and from the back of his throat came a fizzing sensation, like electricity.

In a sudden burst a modest jet of flame flew out, falling short of the target, but coming halfway towards it.

Yoshiko's mouth dropped down in amazement. He had done it! He had made fire! Then he looked down at his belly.

To his shock his body was no longer the rich red of the Nephan clan. He had turned bright orange.

Yoshiko gasped, looking to find his arms and legs were glowing the same colour – even his feet throbbed with the new colour.

Then, almost as quickly as he'd noticed it the colour faded, and his body returned to the Nephan red. Yoshiko blinked, and looked again. Cautiously he held out his talons, but they were also back to their deep natural shade. His immediate thoughts returned back to his fire-breathing achievement and he ran over to Ketu and Kiara.

'I made flames!' he pointed back towards the target. 'I can do it!'

Ketu and Kiara both followed him to the target.

Yoshiko puffed up his chest. The rich warmth in his

belly came, and then the sharp crackle in his mouth, and as they watched he blew out with all his might, and snapped a flicker from his tongue. No fire had emerged, but he had made a spark. 'Great. You're nearly there!' Ketu said.

'Wait!' Yoshiko took hold of Ketu's wing in case he should move. 'I can do more.' He puffed out his chest for another attempt.

This time as he blasted the air forward the spark caught and a tiny but perfect fireball spat forth. Ketu's eyes widened and Kiara clapped her wings.

'And it was even better before. A bigger ball. I need to practise more.' He spread his claws wide to demonstrate.

'Not tonight. Come and eat,' said Kiara. 'School again tomorrow!'

At the thought of the return to Fire School and facing Igorr, Yoshiko's face dropped.

He returned to the front of the cave where the food was laid out. Recalling his colour change he wondered if he should now mention it but as Kiara and Ketu bit into the soft warm pie he did not wish to disturb their look of contentment.

Yoshiko glanced down at his red claws and concluded that he had just imagined the rush of orange colour.

5

Flying High

'Come on, Yoshiko!' Ketu huffed very early one morning. 'Time for a flying lesson! We shall spend the morning practising at the flying rock!'

Yoshiko looked back at him warily, the remains of his breakfast still on his muzzle.

He had filled out, Ketu had noticed, during his first few months of Fire School. Ketu hoped that the fire-training exercise would do him good, knowing that Kiara fed their son so many treats.

Yoshiko loved dragon puffs, a sweet sticky delicacy found in the centres of bulbous flowers from the Mida clan forests. Yoshiko had plumped out thanks to these sugary snacks that he loved to toast in their cave fire until they were crunchy. This gave Igorr and his friends even more reason to laugh at him at school.

* * *

'By the time we get back you won't need to travel with me to school any more,' Ketu declared. 'I'm taking you to a special rock where I learned to fly at your age,' he continued encouragingly. 'No one should be there but us. You can practise all you want freely.'

His son climbed aboard, and with a wave from Kiara they were soon airborne, floating through the mists of Dragor. Ketu gave an expert sweep of his wing and brought them east, taking them out towards the dragons' Burial Ground where he could see the faded Red Seventh Moon seasonal tributes left to honour the dead.

They cruised closer to a large rock under which a river ran, and Ketu landed, folding his huge wings under himself. Yoshiko hopped off his back and gazed in awe over the edge. The waters beneath them looked calm and still, but it was a long way down.

'Is this where I try?' he asked.

Ketu nodded. 'This is where my elder brought me to practise and his elder before him. Most clans have their own special flying rock.'

As he spoke a sudden gust of wind made them both look up. Gandar landed heavily beside them both with Igorr staring smugly, seated on his back.

'I see you're in my son's flying-practice spot,' said Gandar, eyeing Yoshiko with obvious derision. 'How funny that you've brought a hatchling not yet ready to fly.'

Ketu tried to reply calmly, though Yoshiko noticed a vein in his neck was throbbing. 'You know this is my clan's training location,' he replied. 'The Nephans have always had this rock and other clans have honoured that since we all came to Dragor.' Ketu paused as if to reflect on his own words then continued. 'But at the last Council gathering I attended our leader Kinga insisted upon friendship and sharing amongst all clans. So I shall respect that and welcome you to share the rock.'

Gandar threw his head back haughtily.

'Such gracious words, Ketu! But let me tell you this. I will use whichever flying rock I want whenever I want with your permission granted or not. My youngling Igorr already far excels your son at fire breathing, and he shall be far better in all his dragon skills. In fact I see no reason why we should have to waste time watching your hopeless little dragon,' he made a scornful motion with his wings. 'Yoshiko will be falling in the water all day,' scoffed Gandar. 'I doubt he can fly at all.'

Ketu's eyes suddenly flashed fire and Gandar raised himself even higher on his haunches, clearly enjoying the effect he was having on the other adult dragon.

'You Nephan clan dragons think you have a right to everything just because one of your kind is voted as Dragor leader,' he continued. 'Just because Surion and his father Goadah led us to Dragor you now think the red dragons are better at taking charge of the clans. Every dragon knows the purple Alanas have the greatest stamina in the skies. It should be us who make the decisions and rule right now.'

Ketu did all he could not to retaliate. He had heard the same argument so many times before. This strain of bitterness was well known in Dragor. Many of the Alana clan felt that the Nephans had ruled for too long, and that their own kind should have a chance as leaders, rather than simply acting as catchers of fish. But the Council knew that the rebellious Alanas would cause more problems than they solved if given the task of ruling, and for decades had voted to keep Kinga in rule, a red Nephan.

'Where our sons learn to fly has nothing to do with Nephan leadership or anything else,' replied Ketu. 'You know that this is our ancestors' flying place, and today we landed before you did, but again I repeat that, since the clans must get along in Dragor I am happy to share the rock.'

Igorr hopped down from his elder's back looking not the least bit embarrassed at the scene. 'Let's practise over here,' he said, pulling at his elder's wing and pointing to an area on the other side of the rock. 'Away from Feddy.' His elder nodded. 'As you wish, Igorr.' Then they moved over to the far side.

Ketu looked down at Yoshiko inquisitively as Igorr called him by the nickname, but the younger dragon only shrugged.

'It's the name that the Alanas all call me at school,' he murmured, trying to sound as if he didn't care, but the look on his elder's face pained him enough that tears rose up. Yoshiko turned away to hide his face, as a strange feeling started rising in his stomach. It reminded him a little of the time he'd first blown fire but it wasn't a warm glow that he felt, but something thick and dark.

Taking a deep breath Yoshiko tried to shake the feeling away, but it stayed rooted inside him.

'See the river below?' asked Ketu, pointing down with his wing. 'This keeps you safe. It looks like a long way down, but the distance is helpful. You will need to get plenty of air under your wings.'

He noticed his son's anxious face. 'Don't worry, the worst thing that can happen is you will hit the water!'

Yoshiko looked over to Igorr and saw the purple dragon was staring at him mockingly. Then suddenly, Igorr dropped like a stone over the edge of the rock. The beating of air could be heard and a few seconds later Igorr crested triumphantly up into the sky. He flapped low over the rock for a moment, and then sank back to his elder's side.

'Did you see?' crowed Gandar. 'My point has been proved to you. We Alanas are the best! Yoshiko will never fly as well as Igorr.' He turned back to his son. 'Show them again,' he said. 'Take another flight.'

Igorr looked scared for a moment. 'My wings need a rest,' he said. 'I don't know if I can make it a second time so soon.'

Gandar looked angrily at him. 'Do it again, Igorr. Do it now!' he ordered. 'Stop complaining.' And with that he pushed Igorr back towards the edge. The look of triumph had gone from his son's face as he spread his wings again and threw himself from the edge.

This time there was a much longer pause before he rose, and when finally Igorr's purple wings drew him above the rock his face had paled from its deep violet shade. He barely managed to rise above the edge of the rock, and then dropped, throwing a single wing on to the ledge to save himself before hauling his large body over.

Gandar's expression was stony as his son tried to right himself panting and sweating with the exhaustion. He turned away from him in disgust. 'Useless,' he hissed. 'You are simply not trying, Igorr. I could do so much better at your age.'

The intense feelings that Yoshiko had been fighting now grew to a peak. He unfurled his own wings and charged towards the end of the rock, flinging into the empty air.

He descended, feeling the rush of cool water racing up to meet him, his wings beat without him thinking about it, and in a moment he was rising into the air. It almost felt too easy. Yoshiko flapped again, and the motion sent him spiralling up far higher than Igorr had done.

Feeling free and joyous he let the natural shape of his body lean against the sky, with the breeze billowing beneath him he coasted on the air as he'd watched Ketu do so many times before. He stretched them out as wide as he could and made a large and graceful circle over the rock.

Yoshiko took a quick look below, expecting to see Ketu looking up proudly at him, but to his surprise all the figures on the rock were staring with horror.

Disconcerted he brought his wings inwards, wheeling unsteadily down, and landing in a clumsy tumble on the floor.

Ketu ran towards him and caught him up in his wings.

'Yoshiko, what's wrong with you?' he asked. 'What's happened to your scales?'

Yoshiko shook his head in confusion, seeing that both Igorr and Gandar were also looking over at him in alarm.

'What is wrong with your son, Ketu?' asked Gandar, sounding frightened. 'He has turned Alana.'

Yoshiko looked down to see to his horror that it had happened again. He had changed colour. This time he was glowing purple, from head to toe.

6

The Herb Doctor

'Yoshiko, is it?' said the dark blue dragon with huge silver spectacles hanging from his pointy snout. 'Come inside.'

Kiara and Yoshiko stood up to enter the doctor's cave.

The Herb Doctors had the huge task of keeping the dragons of Dragor healthy, treating ailments like sore throats, backache and broken claws. Many dragons were given specially prescribed herb potions to cure their illnesses.

As they followed the doctor, Yoshiko stared at the hundreds of jars of herbs that filled the shelves of his cave. Many sets of crystal wands hung from the ceiling like icicles.

'Come sit before me, youngling,' said the doctor looking over his glasses. 'What seems to be the problem?'

'We don't know what to make of it,' Kiara said. 'My son seems to be changing colour. When he was learning to fly he changed from red to purple, and he has just told us that when he first blew fire, a similar thing happened, but that time thought he turned orange.'

'Never heard of this before,' the doctor replied. He reached his arm up and selected a particularly long crystal. He then began tapping it against Yoshiko's chest, listening intently.

He nodded, took out a charcoal stick, made some notes on his slate and then drew out the hatchling's wings as wide as they could go. 'Take a deep breath,' he said. 'Now again.'

Yoshiko obeyed, letting his wings rise and fall.

The doctor dropped them back down again, and pulled out a small torch from his desk that he lit with a small puff of fire. He shone the light into Yoshiko's eyes and ears. Finally he had him step on to a set of scales, and wrote down the numbers.

'Well. It's all pretty clear to me,' he said finally, settling back down on to his haunches. Kiara looked anxious.

'There is nothing medically wrong with your son,' said the doctor. 'His vital signs are healthy, and his general physical form is good,' he continued, eyeing Yoshiko. 'But his wings are strangely made for a Nephan and will take some adjusting to,' he added. 'Very large and not so nipped-in at the sides as you might expect; in fact they are the biggest wings I have ever seen on a dragon his age.'

The doctor tapped the underside of Yoshiko's wings.

'Some odd scales here too,' he said, pointing. 'These seem like they haven't quite joined up with the rest of him.'

Yoshiko had never noticed before, but could now see that he had many ridges that looked like hooks, hanging away from the wing rather than lying flat as they were supposed to. He closed his wings self-consciously.

'If you don't like the look of them I can clip them off,' said the doctor.

He made a cutting motion with his talon. Kiara shook her head and gasped loudly.

'Then just leave them be,' he continued, catching her expression.

The doctor put his equipment back into his desk and sat back.

'One thing is for sure though – he clearly is overfed,' he said, pointing towards Yoshiko's rounded stomach. 'All things added together probably make him all the more keen to prove himself with the other dragons.'

Kiara tried to reassure Yoshiko by laying her arm on top of his.

'You are seeing the scales lose a little of their colour,' said the doctor looking at Yoshiko directly. 'You say you went orange when you were making fire? And purple in the presence of some Alana dragons?' he continued. 'I expect what you saw was the reflection of the fire itself on your scales, and the second occasion, well, you were by a river which may have reflected the light back on to you.'

Kiara looked bewildered. 'I am informed by his father that he definitely went purple,' she said.

The doctor shook his head dismissively. 'He is perfectly healthy.'

'Doctor, there are several witnesses of these colour changes!' insisted Kiara.

But the doctor wasn't listening. 'Come back to me only if there is something serious. I have no time for trivial issues,' he said, signalling the conversation was closed.

Yoshiko hopped down off the desk and Kiara rushed him out of the door.

'Come on,' she said, throwing her wing around him, 'let's go home and toast you some dragon puffs on the fire.'

7

Colour Change

During the seasons that followed, Yoshiko learned to accept that he could sometimes change colour, but did his best to hide it from his classmates at Fire School. He found that he changed colour more often when he was upset and he strove to keep his feelings from spilling out into his scales.

Igorr had tried to spread the word about what he had seen at the flying rock, but to Yoshiko's relief the idea seemed too strange for the others to believe him.

All of the younglings were improving their skills. Yoshiko could now fly all the way to school, and he and Amlie went together, relishing the freedom of the skies. As their elders had instructed, however, the younger dragons never flew over Cattlewick Cave, taking the longer route to avoid the solitary mountain.

They often tried to guess who or what the mysterious dragon Guya might be. Their vivid imaginations had concluded together that he must at the very least have super-strength.

'Maybe he mixes up potions for dragons to give them more vivid dreams,' said Yoshiko as they flew to school one morning. 'Perhaps he has special eyesight and swims to the depths of the Great Waters by night, gathering glitter-fish to decorate his cave. And maybe on the top of his head is a huge metal horn for him to burrow through rocks,' he added.

They'd long since exhausted the general rumour about Guya, which was that he must have broken some law, making him a bad dragon.

At school they trained every day to make fire, Amlie had taught herself to blow complicated shapes through each nostril, and though Igorr taunted him for his lack of talent as a fire-blower Yoshiko could now at least make basic flames.

Yoshiko and Amlie had made new friends: a female dragon from the Mida clan with large dark brown eyes called Cindina, and a triple-horned male dragon named Elsy from the Effram clan. Both Cindina and Elsy had warned Yoshiko of a mean joke that Igorr and his friends had attempted to play on him by moving the target further away during their fire practice and they had been friends ever since.

The four dragons now regularly ate their midday meal together.

'What do you think about doing some Fire Pit training soon?' asked Elsy one day, as they munched on handfuls of stone-baked chips washed down with sorrel juice. 'We have toughened our scales from the heat made during fire-making practices and none of us need whale-fruit for protection any more.'

Yoshiko looked out wistfully to the Fire Pit at the front of the Fire School entrance where he could make out the peak of the flames that heated the cave to red-hot temperatures.

'The Fire Pit is just full of Alanas,' he replied in a fearful tone.

Elsy shook his head. 'Not only Alanas,' he said. 'Other clans go there too.'

Yoshiko was silent. He knew what Elsy was about to suggest.

'We should try it out now,' Elsy announced. 'Let's try

walking in the big Fire Pit. We can't be scared off by Igorr and his crew.'

Amlie gulped down her juice in excitement.

Yoshiko looked at Elsy's scales, which were shiny and somewhat toughened. Yoshiko knew that Elsy had been exposed to the intense heat from the pot-making furnaces in his clan. He examined his own softer covering.

'Come on, Yoshiko.' Amlie was on her feet and tugging him up eagerly. Cindina looked worried. 'I'm not coming,' she said, looking warily at Yoshiko as if to warn him away. 'I hate the feeling of so much heat. Besides, I want to keep my scales smooth.' She tapped her delicate orange-coloured skin.

Elsy took hold of Yoshiko's wing. 'Come on, Yoshiko!' he said. Looking at his friends' eager faces, Yoshiko didn't know what to do. Cindina was already retreating back to the school entrance.

'OK, then,' he said reluctantly. 'But don't blame me if we all suffer the scale-aches tonight.'

'No chance,' said Elsy as he raced off towards the Fire Pit, fanning out his wings to move him faster as he went.

With a delighted look at Yoshiko, Amlie copied him,

running across the main crescent making a squealing sound.

The Fire Pit loomed on the other side of the crescent and today appeared particularly dark and sinister-looking.

Igorr and his friends were standing near to it, and when they saw Yoshiko a great sneer went up.

'Hey look! If it isn't little Feddy!' said Igorr loudly. 'Don't tell me you've come to show yourself up again and go crying home to your elders?'

'You're no superdragon yourself!' retorted Elsy, narrowing his eyes at Igorr. 'You're not yet walking into the fire and I can see you're still using whale-fruit on your ears. In my clan even the babies don't need such a thick coating of protection.'

Igorr frowned, and Yoshiko noticed, even though he stood some distance away, that his purple ears were indeed dripping with the tell-tale fruit.

'It's true, it's true, look at that jelly dripping every-where,' shouted one of Igorr's friends loudly. Cries of laughter rang out and Igorr's embarrassment seemed to make the whale-fruit run down his face even more.

Igorr looked towards some of the older Alana dragons at the Fire School, wondering if they would take an interest in defending a youngster from their own clan. But the burly dragons were too preoccupied, striding purposefully towards the hottest depths of the pit, every muscle on their faces in concentration, sweat pouring from their snouts.

'I'd like to see you do it better as you are so full of yourself,' Igorr finally retorted. Elsy grinned, and dropped his school net to the ground by Amlie. 'You just watch me!' With that Elsy walked calmly to the Fire Pit entrance and strode a good way into it.

He emerged triumphant with only the slightest trickle of sweat on his upper lip as the crowd cheered.

Igorr set his mouth meanly. 'Now I'd like to see Feddy here walk the same path,' he said. 'The little Nephan has had so little contact with fire – look at his skin.'

Yoshiko looked back at him, desperately trying to stay calm. He felt the sensation he always got before he changed colour and the last thing he wanted was all the dragons present to see him transform.

'It's not a competition, Igorr,' he said. 'I didn't come here to wage a war of words with you, and you know that no other dragons have the naturally hardened scales of the Effram clan, which Elsy comes from.'

Igorr's mouth opened in a delighted smile as he

regained full confidence. 'Awww. What a shame. He is afraid!' he chanted. 'Thinks he can stand there and watch me being mocked. The loser has come to walk the Fire Pit and now he is too frightened!'

Amlie barged forward as best she could, puffing her tiny chest out. 'He is not frightened to do anything you could do, Igorr,' she said. 'You couldn't walk the same route that Elsy just managed. You are nothing but a sad, mean, nasty bully. Leave Yoshiko alone to walk the fire his own way and when he is ready.'

By now most of the older dragons had stopped their own practice and grouped to watch the argument escalate between the younglings. Some had even sat down to watch as they cooled down out of the fire.

Seizing the opportunity to humiliate Yoshiko further, Igorr began to chant. 'Walk! Walk! Walk! Come on! Show us you can manage to walk into the Fire Pit!'

Igorr's friends joined in and then some of the crowd followed. Something inside Yoshiko began to fizz, and to his horror he realised he was changing colour. His talons were tinged yellow, and he knew that soon the shade would wash over his entire body.

Yoshiko blinked his eyes as he willed the colour to go away with all his heart, but instead he felt the sensation rising further and did the only thing he could think to do in the circumstances. He spread his wings and launched himself into the air, putting as much distance between himself and the Fire School as possible.

As he rose he could hear Igorr's taunts were loud and more victorious. As he turned, leaving the school far behind him, he looked down at his body to see that he had changed bright yellow like the sun.

Before Yoshiko could help himself large tears began to fall, he flew on and on with blurred vision before finally landing untidily on a distant mountain. He tried to take a deep breath to calm down, but no calmness came, and instead he felt himself entirely overwhelmed with despair.

'My life is pointless,' he said suddenly to himself, wondering at how true it all sounded when he said it out loud. A torrent of anger took hold of Yoshiko and he began pacing up and down. 'I was the last in my clan to breathe fire,' he said, as if checking off a list of his failures. 'I am heavy and clumsy. I have stupid supersized wings, and now everyone at Fire School thinks I am a total coward.'

More tears fell as he considered the unfairness of everything. What had he done to Igorr and his friends to deserve their treatment of him? The idea of isolation at one of Dragor's many distant outposts appealed to him.

'There is no happiness ahead for me,' he said, before collapsing back down on his haunches with a heavy sigh.

To his great surprise his lament was met with an answer.

'What are you doing here?'

Raising himself up cautiously, Yoshiko rubbed away the tears and peered out into the distance. There he saw the outline of a dragon carrying a basket of freshly picked herbs and roots.

'Who are you?' asked Yoshiko, alarmed to see an elder on this deserted mountain. As the dragon drew closer it was without doubt the strangest sight he'd ever seen. Yoshiko noticed that his horns were thick and greying to suggest a great age, but unlike most elders this dragon had pronounced muscles all over his body, and the glistening turquoise eyes of a newborn. His scales were a deep ocean-blue, some rising in rows as if to form waves. He looked completely different from others of the Saiga clan, as if he was of an entirely different species.

'Surely you have heard of me?' asked the dragon. 'This is my mountain, after all. I am Guya.'

8

Guya

Yoshiko backed away with uncertainty.

'I – I am sorry,' he said, remembering the rule to keep away from Guya's mountain. 'I didn't mean to land *here*. I'll leave you. Leave you alone right now.'

'Go then,' said Guya. 'Run away if you like. I have no time for smallings anyway. Especially a smalling who is ungrateful for his good fortune and feels sorry for himself.'

The old dragon had turned and began to plod away in the direction he had come from.

Yoshiko felt annoyed by his words. No dragon used the old-fashioned expression smalling any more, and he felt angry at how the older dragon seemed to be making fun of him.

'I'm not ungrateful,' he said to Guya's retreating back. 'Things are not easy for me!'

To his surprise Guya stopped and inclined his ageing head.

'Oh?' he said. 'And just what is it that is so difficult for you?'

Yoshiko was unable to stop his tears from welling up again. 'I am the worst at Fire School!' he blurted. 'I can't really do anything well that a dragon like me should be able to do! And other dragons at Fire School make me feel bad.' Yoshiko stuck out his lower lip in grief at the thoughts.

Guya remained standing still but did not turn around.

'Nothing life-threatening then,' he said. 'And no one can make you feel bad, without you allowing them to.' Guya began to shuffle off again and called over his shoulder, 'All this crying over nothing.'

Yoshiko watched him go, feeling the misery settle back around him.

He mouthed after Guya, thinking the old dragon was too far away to hear the words.

'I change colour too,' he whispered to himself. 'I change colour like a chameleon.'

It felt like a great relief to say it, even if no one heard.

Immediately, Guya stopped in the distance and turned around.

He settled his turquoise eyes on Yoshiko and paused for a long moment. Then he motioned with his claw.

'Come,' he said. 'Follow me.'

Yoshiko looked at him uncertainly.

'Follow. Follow.'

Guya grunted in impatience and beckoned with his claw again. Yoshiko obeyed, moving quickly to keep up with the old dragon as he disappeared into the distance.

They rounded the mountain path and a large craggy entrance revealed itself, far grander than Yoshiko's family cave. He stared up in wonder at the lofty opening.

'Now stop and wait here!' Guya motioned that Yoshiko should stay at the mouth of the cave. He stood nervously. A smell was coming from the entrance. Yoshiko recognised it as the scent of sorrel juice, but it was more exotic and powerful than he had smelt before. A strange whirring noise followed as though a heavy door had been opened.

After waiting for a few minutes Yoshiko's nerves vanished and he began wondering what Guya was doing inside. He couldn't hear the old dragon and was beginning to think he had forgotten him entirely.

Shifting forward slightly, Yoshiko moved so he could peer along the length of the cave entrance.

It was dimly lit and he could hardly see anything except for the long, white candle that Guya was holding. It lit a small room that the old dragon had entered.

Yoshiko continued to move forward and he could make out Guya's haunches. He was settled as though he was looking at something inside the rocky mountain. Yoshiko leaned further.

Guya was using a single talon to trace something on the cave wall. Something like . . . pictures. Yoshiko strained to see. It looked as though colourful paintings of dragons had been etched into Guya's dwelling. But there were some other creatures that Yoshiko had never seen before.

Yoshiko squinted to see. They were much smaller than the dragons, and their shape was different.

Humans, Yoshiko realised suddenly.

Guya's talon was tapping a picture thoughtfully.

Yoshiko strained to get an even better look. Then the old dragon sat up suddenly, and Yoshiko moved quickly back outside the cave, anxious about what he had seen.

Surely dragons were not allowed pictures of humans in their caves?

He heard Guya shuffle away from the cave wall, but it was several more minutes before his blue scales came into view again at the entrance. Gripped in his claws was a steaming cup of sorrel juice.

Yoshiko watched as the steam from it swirled in patterns like ghosts in the air.

'Come,' said Guya, without bothering to explain himself. 'This way.'

Guya set off ahead and Yoshiko had to work to keep up. As he rounded the corner the old dragon was already vanishing around another curve of the large mountain.

Yoshiko chased behind, not looking where he was going in his haste to keep up, and as he hurried round the corner where Guya had disappeared, he smacked bodily into the bulk of the other dragon.

'Look,' Guya said slowly, 'where you are going!' Then with an elegant sweep of his talons he gestured out before him as if making an introduction.

Yoshiko looked out in awe at the Great Waters before him. From this part of Dragor the waters glinted as if they were filled with gold as the sun's intensity penetrated through the mist of smoke that rose from the Fire Which Must Never Go Out. The sweep of the liquid seemed endless. He whistled appreciatively and for the first time Guya chuckled.

'There may be greatness ahead for Dragor,' he said, 'if a dragon can master his gifts.'

'From this angle it makes the water appear so magical,' breathed Yoshiko.

'The Great Waters are stunning from many different points. Here you are looking at them in a different way. Very few dragons stop to look. Their lives are so busy it is as if they become blind and never truly open their eyes.'

Guya lifted up his cup of sorrel juice.

'Many dragons have forgotten the proper way to make sorrel juice,' he said as the fragrances spread. 'Always in a rush, looking for a shortcut in so many aspects of life,' he said. 'The old ways are the best.' As if to prove this he took a long gulp with a happy sigh and eyed the younger dragon.

Yoshiko relaxed in the sun's warmth as he took in the beautiful view over the waters. A slow steady heat seemed to build in his feet and it began to rise through him steadily.

Yoshiko concentrated harder and the luxurious

feeling passed all over, rippling from his forehead to the claws of his feet.

Then he looked down at his body.

His red colour was being washed over with a dark blue; he was turning the same shade as Guya from head to toe. Yoshiko gasped in horror.

Guya looked at him and simply nodded. 'It is just as I thought.' Then he rose to his feet as if no more would be said on the subject, and began to walk back to the entrance of his cave.

Yoshiko scrambled after him.

'Wait!' he cried, as Guya rounded the curve in the mountain. 'I need your help!'

Guya stopped and turned. 'So your scales keep changing colour, little dragon!'

'Yes,' said Yoshiko. 'And I would do anything to discover why the colour change happens and stop it!'

'Likely you will never be able to change what you are,' said Guya with a grunt.

Yoshiko's face fell and his green eyes peered right into Guya's. 'Please, Guya,' he begged. 'The Herb Doctors down in the valley couldn't help me; you are a Saiga dragon like them but you are supposed to be extra wise. Surely you can help me?'

Guya paused for a moment, his face softening for the first time. 'Yoshiko, consider that these dragons pick on you because there is something about you that they want to take away. As for your colour change, well, there may be a solution!'

Yoshiko felt a sudden flush of relief.

But Guya's face had lost some of its warmth again. He turned away from Yoshiko, and began walking back into his cave.

'It won't be easy, in fact I doubt you are up to it at all,' he said, disappearing into the cave entrance.

Yoshiko shuffled into the cave straight after him but to his surprise Guya was standing upright in the entrance to prevent him from entering further.

Yoshiko tried to keep his voice steady.

'I need answers!' he said.

Guya rested a wing on the younger dragon's shoulder. 'I sense many things about you, Yoshiko, but right now you are too weak in your mind and body to do what is needed to find your answers...'

Suddenly, Yoshiko felt a twinge under his wing and reached under one of his scales. Heat from the stone the Ageless Ones had given him was burning in his side.

'Guya, have you ever seen something like this before?' he asked, holding out the stone.

Guya took the jewel in his claws and brought it closely to his eyes as if inspecting it under a microscope. He straightened up quickly.

'Oh my! The Dancing Opal!' he exclaimed. 'Legend has it that there is just one of these exact stones. It is a callstone!'

'A callstone?' enquired Yoshiko.

'It is a translucent opal and inside it are genies said to help enhance the powers of the twin dragons,' answered Guya. 'I had a vision that one day they would speak again – to foretell some great future event and give the callstone to a dragon, so they can summon their great magic when needed.'

Yoshiko's eyes grew wide as he looked closely at the stone again and could indeed see the tiny genie-like creatures that he thought were just pretty sparkles.

'Where did you get the stone?' Guya asked.

'I was given it at the marketplace,' replied Yoshiko.

Guya was silent for a moment and then went on as though there'd been no sight or mention of the stone.

'Come back here early tomorrow and I shall give you a set of tasks to complete. But I warn you they are more difficult than you can ever imagine.' With that, he gave a wide flick of his tail, and vanished into the back of his cave.

9

The Three
Tasks

The next morning Yoshiko got up before the sun rose to fly out to Guya's cave. 'Where are you going?' asked Ketu sleepily, eyeing his son pushing down a bowl of peat porridge as fast as he could.

'Off to do some practice,' said Yoshiko. 'I heard some from school do early training so they have a better chance of being Guard Dragons.'

'I remembered doing something similar at your age,' Ketu replied smiling. 'Don't give yourself scale-ache, Yoshiko,' he said, presuming he was off to the Fire Pit.

Having finished his breakfast, Yoshiko stretched his wings and launched off into the dark morning.

He had never been out of the cave this early, and the air of Dragor's dawn was refreshing as it rushed over his wings. Already some of the Alana dragons were at fishing spots on the edge of the Great Waters, eager to bring in the best catch of the day.

Yoshiko wheeled in the sky, taking in the various scenes as he headed for Cattlewick Cave.

He landed to find that Guya was already waiting outside for him.

'Good morning, Yoshiko. I have your three tasks to give to you.'

'I am ready for them,' Yoshiko replied, trying to sound braver than he felt.

To his surprise Guya started laughing. 'They cannot be completed in a morning, little dragon,' he said. 'In fact there is a big chance that you will never achieve them!'

He beckoned with his gnarled claw.

'Follow me,' he said. 'I will show you the first.'

Obediently, Yoshiko trotted after Guya to the right side of the cave.

Guya pointed to a large pot. It rested on the ground directly beneath the outer rock face.

'This is a very special pot!' Guya announced.

In front of Yoshiko was an enormous red clay vessel. It was almost as big as he was.

'Into this pot comes rain straight from the sky, it pours in through a hole in the rock,' explained Guya. 'It is special water, very pure to make exceptional sorrel juice.'

Yoshiko eyed the big pot with concern.

'Your first task,' said Guya, 'is to lift that pot. But that time will be long from now,' he added, his gaze dropping.

'Let me try!' said Yoshiko.

Guya shrugged. 'Then try.'

Yoshiko approached the pot curiously. The red clay was nothing he had ever seen before, the outer coating was as if it had formed its own scales.

Yoshiko bent down and flinging his arms around the pot, he made a loud heaving sound as he tried to stand. But the vessel didn't even wobble.

He tried again, this time using every ounce of strength in his body, and a bead of sweat rolled down his face.

Again the pot didn't move a bit.

Yoshiko looked up to see that Guya was grinning.

'As I said, you are not strong enough, little dragon,' he said. 'That is called a Goadah Pot. I imagine you have never seen one before.'

'No, I haven't,' Yoshiko replied. 'Although I have

heard of them. Kiara told me a story when I was younger called "The Magic Goadah Pot".'

Guya nodded. 'Yes, a very popular tale. Now, as you see, the pots actually do exist in real life too, although their magical powers are doubted by many,' he said. 'There are only a few of these pots in Dragor; each one is unique and very precious, and as you witnessed they are even heavier than they look,' he added. 'This one was made just after the Battle of Surion. You are clearly far from ready to lift this pot. Maybe in three winters you will, little one.'

Yoshiko was outraged. 'I'll have been laughed out of Fire School by that time.'

Guya shrugged. 'If you want to spend your days feeling sorry for yourself it could be ten winters.'

'What are the other tasks?' Yoshiko asked impatiently.

Guya smiled. 'The other tasks are equally difficult.'

He extended a talon to count off on three claws. 'First, the little dragon must be strong enough to lift the Goadah Pot. Second, the little dragon must have the wing strength to fly around Dragor seven times.'

'Seven times?'

Guya nodded and Yoshiko felt his heart sink. Only the fittest Guard Dragon could do so much flying.

'What is the third task?' he asked, the dejection sounding in his voice.

'For the third task, you must stand in a fire pit of my making for the time it takes a cauldron of sorrel juice to boil.'

Yoshiko was horror-struck. It sounded impossible. He had no idea how he could ever be strong enough to lift the pot, let alone fly around Dragor seven times, but he felt a burning need to prove Guya wrong.

'I told you it would be difficult! If I were you I would just not bother trying these tasks! They are great challenges, clearly too great for you,' said Guya, but there was a certain sparkle in his eye as he said it.

'I shall complete your tasks,' said Yoshiko firmly. 'And I'll be back sooner than you think!'

With that he spread his wings to head for Fire School. 'Oh, and one more thing, Guya,' Yoshiko added. 'Perhaps when I return you will be so kind as to stop calling me a little dragon!'

As Yoshiko flew off Guya chuckled to himself.

10

Training with Romao

Yoshiko was pondering about his first challenge, how he could become strong enough to lift Guya's pot, and an idea came to him unexpectedly.

Ketu and Kiara were reminiscing about Yoshiko's birth and were discussing their former Guard Dragon Romao who had just that week been awarded a promotion.

'I always knew that dragon, Romao, would go far,' said Ketu to Kiara. 'When I saw him over ten years ago in that spear-throwing contest I knew that I must select him to be our cave guard during Yoshiko's nesting period. In fact there and then I would have bet fifty glass stones that he would have made it to a senior guard like he just has.'

Yoshiko had only met his former Guard Dragon a few times, but he knew that Romao looked upon him like a little brother, having been there to protect him at the family cave during his hatching.

'Do you think Romao would train me?' Yoshiko asked Ketu suddenly.

'You want personal training from one of the best Guard Dragons in Dragor! I expect you'll be outdoing me at fire and flying soon.' He looked delighted at his son's request.

Kiara, as usual, responded with concern. 'It is because of those Alana dragons picking on you, isn't it?' she declared. 'Yoshiko, I do not want you training so you can start fights. We must deal with it another way.'

Ketu turned the warmth of his smile on her. 'Kiara, my dear, please do not assume the worst. Romao will train him only so he can improve his skills, and it will be a benefit if he can protect himself should the need arise. I'll have a message sent to Romao straight away.' Ketu put a big spoon of Kiara's homemade sticky mash into his mouth. 'My son,' he continued, 'training with the Guard Dragons. What a proud elder I am.'

*　*　*

The next day Romao was waiting to meet Yoshiko after Fire School and Igorr and his friends saw him.

'Need a Guard to escort you home?' mocked Igorr, as Yoshiko headed towards Romao.

Romao, hearing the taunts, began to wander towards Yoshiko and Igorr backed away.

Yoshiko tried to force a smile as Romao approached and patted him with a friendly wing.

'Ketu tells me you want to train with me?' said Romao.

Yoshiko nodded. 'I want to get strong, fly far, and become heat resistant . . .' he paused as he looked at his plump body and then continued, 'I need to be able to lift really heavy things like big pots. I know right now it is hard to believe.'

Romao smiled warmly as he looked at Yoshiko's overhanging belly.

'Ambition is great, Yoshiko, and indeed I am the right person to help you, but we must take it one step at a time. Have you yet managed any of the flight paths at the Trail Mountains?'

Yoshiko shook his head. 'I stay away from the Alana territory.'

'Well, we'll start first with training your wings in

preparation,' said Romao. 'Lifting clay discs, and fan-beating the flames. That should be enough to give you the strongest wings of any dragon your age in Dragor!' he added encouragingly.

'Follow me,' he said, and took to the skies, heading towards the Guard Dragons' training grounds. He then picked up some speed and took Yoshiko for a faster flight, circling all of the Alana Mountains.

Romao spotted several Guard Dragons who were prowling around the Trail Mountains, and started to descend. He landed, shortly followed by Yoshiko, who was out of breath and panting.

Romao looked at his little chest moving in and out.

'The secret to becoming a Guard Dragon is practise, practise, practise,' he said, as they watched the guards swoop at high speeds over their heads. 'See that dragon there?' He pointed to a blue Talana dragon, whose scales rippled with the muscle underneath. 'He was really clumsy in the air when he started,' said Romao. 'Now he is one of Dragor's best. Every day he trains around the Trail Mountains.'

Several of the passes had been adapted by a team of Guard Dragons and were the pride and joy of their Captain Ayo. He had instructed the trails to be full of flight obstacles and targets so as to help improve the flying skills of any trainees.

Yoshiko looked in awe at some dragons flying into the entrances at breakneck speeds. A Guard Dragon then came swooping down behind them from one of the exits and shot across the Great Waters. Then with absolute precision the dragon smashed a row of clay pots floating on the surface.

As the fragments sank out of sight another dragon at the edge of the Great Waters began turning a pulley system. It ferried another set of pots out into position, waiting for the next dragon.

'You won't be ready for the Trail Mountains until you are very fit,' said Romao. 'One wrong turn and that could be the end of it.'

'Have you ever hit a mountain?' asked Yoshiko.

Romao shook his head. 'No, but I was injured badly when I caught a turn wrong,' he said, unfurling his large wing and showing Yoshiko an ugly raised scar. 'Every year there are one or two dragons who fly the trails too early and hurt themselves. The hardest trail has lava pits along the way that throw smoke and ash up, plus there are jets of scalding water from the rocks that shoot sky high. Go through either of those at the wrong point and it could be fatal.' Romao's tone was serious.

'Come,' he continued. 'Let's fly over the simple adventure course. All you have to do is swing in and out changing sides in order to avoid the trees. You cannot hurt yourself even if you hit the branches as the leaves are soft and cushioning. We will train here every day until you absolutely perfect it, then you can move on.'

They turned and flew at a gentle speed that allowed Yoshiko to fly beside Romao, swinging in and out of the small forest. He sailed through the course with ease.

'Great, let's go see how the Alanas train – the most talented in the air of all the clans,' said Romao.

They approached the Great Waters, Romao cried out against the shrill of the wind, 'Now . . . Look down! See the Alanas are all practising their skills. Watch how they are doing fancy turns before they dive deeply into the water. They are making their bodies and wings as straight as they can. They are challenging themselves to build up a perfect score. Every year at Red Seventh Moon these dragons gather for the Great Races. All the Guard Dragons will be taking part and competing for the main award. I am already training hard for the next one. It's going to be so much fun!'

'Do you really think I could ever make a Guard?' Yoshiko asked hopefully.

Romao turned to him and examined his current form in the skies.

'Most dragons never use all their talent. They don't ever develop the right attitude. Won't listen. Won't learn,' he said. 'They fly only to get around Dragor. If you are willing to train hard there is almost no end to what you can achieve. Wing exercises,' Romao continued, 'are the first essential for improving flight.' He stretched out his large wings and hovered as he pushed them up and down quickly.

'First we train for strength in the wing,' he said.

'Then we train for accuracy. Then one day you will be ready for the Trail Mountains.'

They landed next in the far west of Dragor at the Clay Hills and Romao led Yoshiko into the Guard Dragons' training cave. Loud grunts and the sight of many large dragons greeted them. 'The Guards need to have very strong wings,' Romao said. He hefted up a huge thick disc to show it to Yoshiko. 'See this! One day you will be able to lift one of these with a wing.'

Yoshiko peered at the disc, which looked as if it must be at least half his weight.

'The back area of this cave is where we will train,' said Romao, and he led Yoshiko through into a smaller room.

Here many dragons were gathered, lifting clay discs on their wings, with others placing the discs on and off to help them.

'Good for beginners,' said Romao, pointing to the thinnest disc. 'Very lightweight.'

He indicated where Yoshiko should stand. 'Spread your wings,' he said, and Yoshiko opened his large wings, feeling discomfort at showing his strange scales publicly.

'Hold them down,' said Romao, placing the disc on to the tip of Yoshiko's wing. 'Now, UP!'

Yoshiko lifted his wing easily. 'Good. You have some natural strength,' said Romao. 'So we can try you on a slightly larger disc.' He vanished for a moment, returning with a slightly thicker one.

Romao placed the new disc on to Yoshiko's wing, which shook this time as he tried to raise it, but he mustered all of his strength and managed to lift it. Romao looked pleased. 'Good work! This is the level we'll start you at,' he said. 'Now for the other side.'

* * *

After an hour at the training cave Romao reckoned it was enough for the first session and decided to take him out to a remote area deeper in the hills where a hoard of dragons were working away on their various creations in clay.

Romao led Yoshiko to a large cave. 'Now for another part of your training,' he said.

'To gain good wing strength and accuracy is one thing. That will help you to take corners faster and swoop down quicker when you need to, but these skills are only one part of what makes a good flyer. The most essential thing is stamina. You can be as fast and strong as you like, but without it you won't be able to keep any activity up for long. Stamina is what the winning dragons have – the ones who lead any race track right to the end. A lot of dragons only train for strength,' continued Romao. 'If you have both it will help you greatly.'

They walked down into the hills and towards the huge clay ovens, which were as tall as three dragons. Each was full of a fierce flame and the heat could be felt from far away. In front of the oven was a small

Effram dragon beating the flames with his wings. Romao pointed.

'Do you see that youngling over there?'

Yoshiko nodded, looking at the light green dragon.

'Don't be fooled by his small size. The little fire beaters are the best in long distances out of all of the dragons,' continued Romao. 'We will get your ability to such a level that you can fan flames for hours at a time.'

'Okey-smokey!' Yoshiko clapped his wings together.

'Ready to fan the flames?'

Yoshiko nodded, admiring the little green dragon who stepped aside at a nod from Romao.

Moving into position Yoshiko opened his wings with uncertainty.

'That's the way,' said Romao. 'Now beat them into the fire.' Yoshiko started to pound his wings together, sending gusts of wind towards the flames.

Inside the oven he could see the effect the air was having. It tunnelled down under the logs that had been placed in the oven and charged them with a bright red glow.

'The Efframs want the hot airstream to gush as fast as possible, it fires their clay, making it super hard,'

Romao explained as Yoshiko fanned. 'The clay would not set like rock were it not for the fire beaters.'

Yoshiko was concentrating on his task. He had started quickly, but after only a few minutes found a steady pace.

He continued until he was completely exhausted and his wingbeats began to slow. Romao gestured that the fire beater could return to his job again. The green dragon moved back into place and began beating.

'That was real good,' said Romao. He looked up at the sun. 'By my estimation you kept that up for a full half an hour. Best I have seen from a new starter.' Romao smiled broadly. 'It seems your large wings help your natural stamina.' His eyes dropped to Yoshiko's rounded belly. 'However, one thing at a time. Success depends far more on the will of the dragon. Many dragons start the process but quickly give up.'

'I won't give up,' said Yoshiko quickly. 'I'll train every day.'

'Then, early tomorrow morning we will train again,' said Romao.

Yoshiko agreed.

11

School Lessons

Yoshiko landed at Fire School. After his first two sessions with Romao his wings ached a lot. But he had a strange feeling of satisfaction at what he had achieved. Yoshiko noticed from the empty courtyard that he was one of the first arrivals. He wandered over to the Fire Pit.

'Where's your minder?'

Igorr's voice echoed through the crescent suddenly and Yoshiko's heart sank as he came face to face with his enemy.

'You're just so useless. You can't even do things on your own. You need a minder with you!'

'Leave him alone, Igorr,' said Amlie. Her small body

landed straight between them as if from nowhere. Her intense, tiny blue eyes looked up at Igorr.

Yoshiko went to speak, but instead he turned round to greet Amlie as if Igorr didn't exist.

'Are you deaf?' spat Igorr. Again Yoshiko said nothing, and instead began talking to Amlie about the day's lesson ahead.

'We all know you'll never even make the edges of the Fire Pit,' shouted Igorr as loud as he could, his face filled with rage.

Amlie's face suddenly turned to lightning. With one forceful puff she let out an almighty flame. It caught the back of Igorr's tail and began running up his spine.

'Maybe that will teach you to stop picking on others and calling them names!' she shouted as Igorr screeched, wagging his tail frantically and bashing it on to the dusty ground to put out the fire.

Yoshiko threw his wing around his friend. He realised in that moment that he had been allowing Igorr to take away all of his happiness. 'Come on, Amlie, he is just not worth it!' he said. 'Let's get to class.'

* * *

The history of Dragor was taught by a plump female dragon whose red Nephan scales had turned a dusty pink.

'I bet she never does any fire-walking,' whispered Amlie as they trooped into the cave classroom.

Igorr was now attached to an even meaner-looking group of Alana dragons, who groaned loudly as they came into the class. The room was laid out with small stone desks to allow the dragons to write more easily.

'Who wants to learn about stupid history anyway?' Igorr stated loudly. 'We all already know how to make fire. But then again some people here need lessons,' he continued. 'That Nephan over there definitely needs teaching a lesson or two.' Igorr looked delighted at his words and turned to check that Yoshiko had overheard. His eyes burned with hate.

'Take your places,' called the teacher, the folds of her soft skin rippling as she spoke. She wrinkled up her eyes to peer at the board, and using a stick of charcoal started to write on the board.

'She can't use fire,' whispered Igorr, and the two Alanas sniggered. The teacher whirled around, her tail catching the stone desk making a loud bang that silenced the room.

'I can hear very acutely, however,' she said, glaring at Igorr. 'What is your name, youngling?'

Igorr spelled out his name letter by letter, with a sarcastic grin.

'Igorr with two r's!' repeated the teacher. 'Well, young Igorr, in my class you will learn to stop commenting on other dragons, and become more interested in learning how we dragons came to be in this land.'

She dismissed him with another wave of her tail and Igorr sat down next to his fellow Alanas with his usual frown.

'My name is Ma'am Sancy,' said the teacher, raising her voice to be heard over the class. 'In this class we will learn, not only about the history of Dragor, but further back still, to before we came here. We will learn some very interesting facts,' she added, 'and maybe you little younglings will find out you are not all so different across the clans after all.'

Igorr snorted as if he thought this unlikely and then dropped his head as Ma'am Sancy turned to stare sharply at him.

'I will start with the Battle of Surion. Remember to make notes,' she added. Most of the younglings dug around in their nets to bring out their charcoal sticks and boards and some began to make words on paper with tiny sparks from their dextrous snouts.

'Many great creatures first roamed the earth with us,' Ma'am Sancy announced to her class, her wings held wide. 'There were all different types. Some had trunks and tusks as long as their bodies. Others had claws that enabled them to leap through the highest trees in the forests.' The younglings all gazed at their history teacher, as her words captured their full attention.

'At first they were happy to share the lands with us. But as the years went by, the earth moved and the seas divided,' she continued. 'Some of the dinosaurs sought survival by breeding with our dragon ancestors, creating a super-evil species known as dragsaurs – monsters who were willing do anything to take over the world and destroy us!' One of the orange Mida dragons gasped in horror at the thought of such beasts.

'But despite their efforts, and indeed after many great wars, both dragsaurs and dinosaurs became extinct. It was only us dragons who managed to survive the new climates, though we became slaves to man. That is, until one great rebellion, after receiving a special gift we managed to escape and flee to the Land of Dragor, where we now remain hidden below the smoky mists. But there was a terrible tragedy!'

All the dragons now gasped.

'Surion was killed during a battle. At the foot of our great mountain we fought the humans who had followed us, a spear went through Surion's heart. His elder, Goadah, was heartbroken as his son died. He looked up to the sky and gave out a roaring cry. It was so loud that it caused massive vibrations and the rocks began to break and tumble down the mountain on to the earth. The centre of the mountain then exploded into a hot fiery liquid that poured down like fiery rivers. The rocks and lava from above fell, killing the humans that had pursued, but the dragons entered our valley through a secret entrance and the rocks sealed the entrance securely. The clans then built the Fire Which Must Never Go Out so its smoke will keep us from sight and we are safe if we keep the Goadah rulings. Some say that Surion's heart beats on inside the mountain and protects a precious stone that holds the key to our destiny.'

'That's ridiculous!' said Igorr. 'How can a dragon's heart still live in a mountain? And there is no doubt that Surion of the unusual red egg cursed the clans,' continued Igorr loudly. 'He tricked the dragons into betraying their human masters who used to bring us fish without us even having to work for it. And I rather like the sound of the dragsaurs; they sound powerful and I bet wouldn't have taken any nonsense from stupid red dragons!'

'Better to be free than be a slave, the only stupid thing is wanting to be a slave!' announced Amlie. 'Being a slave means being told what to do. I hate being told what to do. It's far better that we work now for ourselves.'

Ma'am Sancy looked out on to the class as the debate raged.

'My elder says that only foolish dragons believe Surion brought a blessing,' Igorr added. 'The fact is it is all the Nephan clan's fault. If it wasn't for them we would live in our homeland by the seas, and I wouldn't have to put up with living with them when they think they are so special.'

'All clans have equal value,' said Ma'am Sancy. 'I think it is time to move from this Surion topic. Does anyone have a question about the clans?'

It was Amlie who put her arm in the air.

'Ma'am Sancy. Do you know why the yellow Bushki

dragons are the only ones who can make the toffee-nuts grow?'

'Good question, Amlie. Indeed I will tell you this very special story,' she said settling herself. The eyes of the whole class widened.

*   *   *

'A very long time ago, before dragons lived together in this big valley, the clans were scattered all over the world.

The dragon clans all had a love for precious stones, which they would mine from the rocks in their individual lands, and they would use them to decorate their caves, believing they had powers. But the minerals from which these gemstones develop are not found amongst our rocks and only a few stones came into our land; most were left behind.

There are areas outside Dragor that have lots of forests and others that are full of large expanses of open fields. And there are islands too, both small and large lands that sit in the centre of the seas. All the clans developed different talents over time. The purple dragons became fishing types because they come from places with great waters, and the blue Talana dragons who dig under the earth with their powerful horns come from the areas with the rockiest of mountains. As for the red dragons . . .'

'I know this one!' interrupted Amlie. 'We Nephans managed the trades between other clans. And Surion, he was a Nephan!'

Ma'am Sancy continued. 'Yes, and the yellow Bushkis. These dragons now run the book-caves. They keep records of the clans, and continue to record every detail of Dragor history, and whilst our land is cool and surrounded by tall mountains, this country is dry and yellow – the same colour as a Bushki dragon. The forests there are full of many sweet things. Thick treacle drips from the bark of trees and heavenly tasting sticky-fruits burst from the bushes. There are the biggest coconuts too, full of honey-flavoured liquid.' Ma'am Sancy could hear that many of the younglings' stomachs had begun to rumble.

'Legend has it there is one great snake who rules all of these forests. A snake who is as wide as a river and who has teeth as long as a dragon's tail.' Some of the younglings blinked in wonder.

'And they say that when this great snake thumps his

tail three times like this: Thump! Thump! Thump!' – Ma'am Sancy banged her fist three times on the ground '– that the shaking of the earth then makes the toffee-nut trees spring up out of the ground immediately. This special snake can make the nuts appear at any time he chooses in his magical forest.'

'Wow,' said Yoshiko as he checked around the classroom to see that no trees had appeared after Ma'am Sancy's loud thuds. 'Those Bushki dragons were so lucky – imagine being surrounded by nothing but sugary treats. All we have in Nephan forests are sorrel bushes!'

'It's a good job you don't have toffee-nuts in your forests because you would be even fatter than you are now!' Igorr shouted out, making all the Alana young-lings giggle.

'Enough of that. No insults in my class,' Ma'am Sancy warned. 'Or you will be held back after school! Though I am guessing you will choose to be more attentive now, Igorr, when you hear about your own clan.'

Ma'am Sancy began again. 'Long long ago, way before Dragor existed the clans were scattered in the different corners of the world. And it was the Alanas who came from the wettest place, in the north of the world. A place filled with the widest raging rivers that led to oceans far and wide. A place whose lands were veiled with the thinnest grass in the sun season and whose mountains were always topped with ice.'

She looked around the room to see the purple dragons all paying perfect attention.

'Before Dragor came to be, the Alanas lived here in the mountains surrounded by waters in every direction,' said the teacher. 'It is unlike the land of the Efframs which is all of green and plenty, or the milk-and-honey place where the Talanas come from. Here there was little food and the purple dragons were often very hungry. They didn't know then how to fish the oceans and struggled in the harsh climate to scavenge enough to eat. That is until they received a blessing.

'A solitary whale in the ocean became very lonely and grew bored with the tiny fish that surrounded her. She became so sad that she began jumping out of the water. She jumped high into the sky so she could look over the land in search of other large creatures to befriend her. Stronger and stronger she grew as she leapt higher and higher, and her powerful spout shot water out across the sea. As she leapt and snorted she began stirring the ocean like peat porridge in a pot.' Ma'am Sancy's hands began to turn as if she was stirring, and now all the younglings watched her totally transfixed.

'Round and round the whale went, churning and turning, until eventually she made a storm. The waves crashed up into the land, up they went, as high as the mountains and silver fish were thrown up from its depths. The fish landed in the dragon caves and the dragons got a taste for them and decided to learn to hunt for fish. So this is how the Alanas became fishing dragons, and why they now understand the lakes and the seas.

'The whale was finally happy because when the dragons came to hunt for the fish they flew in the skies above her, and then started to dive in the waters with her too. She was entertained by them and it cast away her loneliness.'

The purple dragons all had a look of pride on their faces.

'Over time the Alana have developed noses squeezed in the middle.' Ma'am Sancy made a pinching motion with her claws, and the dragons from the other clans all looked towards the Alanas to see their snouts were indeed thinner in the centre.

'Their noses are perfectly formed to root out the fish

and pull them from the Great Waters, their sharp claws can catch hold of the fish, and if you have a competition to hold your breath with an Alana you'd better watch out! They have big lungs inside those chests and can go without air for longer than any other dragon.'

Igorr looked smug and Amlie rolled her eyes at his expression.

The rest of the day passed by quickly as Yoshiko enjoyed all that Ma'am Sancy taught them. They listened to details about the clay terrain where the artistic Effram clan had come from, and how the dragons had come to shape the clay from the earth. All the younglings were finally set homework – to learn the Dragor Commandments off by heart.

12

The Charcoal Trees

In the weeks of training ahead, Yoshiko spent hours and hours at the Talana adventure course with Romao, practising his turns. They would then fly the circuit around Dragor before going to the dragon gym to work with the weights. These training sessions with Romao had become the best part of Yoshiko's day.

'I've been very proud of your development, Yoshiko,' announced Romao after one particularly intense session. 'You now have good lifting power. But your fire resistance now needs work on it if you ever wish to face the hottest fire pits.'

Yoshiko's gaze fell downwards to his body knowing that Romao was right.

'It is time to take you to a place where there is plenty of heat,' promised Romao. 'Only this time we are going to a different territory.'

Yoshiko wondered what secrets this place might hold as Romao flew him out towards the Burial Ground.

'We are at the edge of Saiga terrain now,' said Romao, 'where it is uninhabited. This area is barren and dry, but one amazing thing does grow here.'

Yoshiko strained his eyes to see the top of the rocks. He could just make out some dark shapes. Then as they drew nearer he realised that the clearings were scattered with dark-grey-coloured trees. They stretched up to the sky like twisted talons.

'Dead trees,' he said, wondering if that was what Romao meant.

The older dragon smiled. 'Not dead at all,' he said. 'Those are charcoal trees and they are still growing. The Herb Doctors make things with special properties from these unique trees. They charm them to grow this way, some of the most powerful charcoal trees are nearly as high as some of the mountains. Just one or two of those twigs could make a whole cave hot for hours. Legend tells it that Surion braved a cave fired by a whole bushel of those charcoal tree branches, and this is where Ayo trains the Guard Dragons.'

They were nearing the trees now, and Yoshiko felt a strong heat in the air and sweat began to run off his face.

'That is the heat the forest naturally gives off as the trees grow. You will feel heat far greater than this as we enter the forest,' said Romao, who was clearly not bothered by the growing temperature. 'Look down there,' he added. 'Below us the Saiga dragons have been planting seeds.' He pointed to where tiny budding twigs were coming from the ground.

The heat was becoming more and more intense, and sweat was now gushing down Yoshiko's snout. Romao stretched his talons to land and Yoshiko copied him, but the heat of the rocks below threw him off balance and he started hopping on the hot rocks.

'Relax your claws,' advised Romao. 'Let them soften into the rock and take the weight off the back of your heels. The heat will not seem so strong.'

Yoshiko released his claws as instructed, trying to brave the heat whilst hopping from one foot to the other. Romao was settling into another lesson.

'The reason why I bought you here, Yoshiko,' he said, 'is that this is the best way to harden your scales. The charcoal tree woods help you in two ways. Firstly, when you cut the wood the heat prepares your lungs for the Fire Pit. Secondly, the fire from these branches when you burn them hardens the scales like nothing else. This wood is another reason the Guard Dragons are so talented. They come here daily to cut the wood and train.'

Yoshiko realised the truth in Romao's statement.

'Come then,' said Romao. 'A few good branches will do it.' They walked inside the forest.

Up close the charcoal trees looked even more eerie. Their branches were knotted and twisted as if disfigured.

'The darkest black trees are the most powerful fire bringers but they resist being pulled down,' said Romao as he reached out to tug down a branch. He dug both claws in and tugged. Eventually the branch snapped free in a shower of black dusty powder.

Yoshiko copied him, taking hold of his own branch he pulled hard. Eventually he snapped off a limb much smaller than Romao's, which felt as heavy as stone.

'Just a few more and we will venture to the pit,' said the older dragon.

* * *

The Fire Pit was lower and narrower than any he had seen elsewhere, and Yoshiko was relieved to see that it had not a single Alana inside. Yoshiko approached with the branches, determined to put every bit of effort into staying in the heat.

Something caught his eye on the outside of the pit. It was a large red clay pot, and it looked exactly like the one in Cattlewick Cave.

They approached an intelligent-looking Saiga dragon at the entrance of the cave, who was busy stoking the flames, and handed over their branches.

'Excuse me. Is that a Goadah pot?' Yoshiko asked, pointing towards it.

'Yes, it is indeed,' replied the dragon. 'One of the last in existence. We keep it here safe and sound. It is regularly fired in the pits to maintain its strength and durability.'

'Is it magical?' asked Yoshiko.

The guard tapped his own muzzle. 'Dragor secret, not something I know about,' he said, winking.

'Can I try to lift it?' asked Yoshiko.

The dragon laughed. 'You can try,' he said. 'But I

know you won't be able to. Many many dragons have tried and failed,' he added.

Yoshiko stepped towards the pot, flexing his wings out, with Romao watching on.

He then threw both wings around the wide pot and heaved with all his might.

'See, I told you so, it didn't even budge,' said the Saiga dragon with assurance.

He then waved them both into the cave.

The first eye-watering wave of heat hit Yoshiko full-force across the face.

In the side areas of the pit were a few Guard Dragons, waiting out the hot temperatures in apparent comfort.

'We'll stay just here now,' said Romao, gesturing they should remain very close to the entrance.

Yoshiko sat down.

With the dark heat of the pit, his mind whirred. How would it be possible to ever lift the Goadah Pot?

He puzzled over the question as his body withstood more and more heat.

13

The Burial Ground

Over the next few months Yoshiko worked as hard as he could. In the mornings he rose early and trained with Romao and in the evenings straight after school he did the same. To his delight he noticed more differences in his body. Muscles started to swell under his scales. Local dragons from the Effram clan lined up to watch Yoshiko beat flames as well as one of their own dragons. Yoshiko could now work for a full day in front of the fires if he chose. Neither did he mind this work.

There was something soothing about pumping the air, forward and continuously, and watching the fire heat the clay.

Collecting the charcoal wood had now built up a stronger resistance to heat, and he had managed the outer areas of the Fire Pit for some length of time though he still pondered daily about the task of lifting Guya's Goadah pot.

*   *   *

He resolved to ask Ketu if he knew more about Guya. So one day, when Yoshiko and his elder were flying back from the marketplace after gathering some supplies, Yoshiko began his questioning.

'Do you know any more facts about Cattlewick Cave?' he asked. His elder turned his head to him and thought for a moment. 'Well, having sat on the Council, I do know more than most, Yoshiko, and I trust you are now old enough for this information to be kept to yourself. Stories often twist over time but the basics of it involves Kinga.' Ketu paused to recall all the details.

'Kinga and Guya were close friends as hatchlings,' he continued. 'Then they were the best of friends all through Fire School and trained hard together to develop their fire skills. Both of them were so talented that they became Guard Dragons at an early age. Then some forty years ago the Council voted Kinga to rule the land and Guya was voted into the Council as representative of the Saiga clan.'

Yoshiko listened attentively.

'At first Guya sat happily by Kinga's side on the Council,' continued Ketu. 'Guya believed in the Dragor rules and made sure that he upheld them,' he said. 'It was very important to him that the Commandments were never questioned. He did everything to ensure all dragons knew of them. Then, one day something happened to change all that.'

Yoshiko leaned closer curiously. 'What happened?'

'In some distant corner of Dragor when he was alone, without any other dragon around, he saw something. It made him question everything and he came to look at our rules differently,' replied Ketu. 'After that he could no longer sit at Kinga's side. He no longer believed in everything he stood for. Though he still believed Kinga a fair ruler.'

Ketu turned slightly on the breeze. 'Guya said that he had to go to some lonely spot and make his own path,' he said. 'At first Kinga tried to persuade him to stay. They argued, but eventually he saw that Guya could not be talked around. To this day Guya has not told

Kinga or any dragon what happened to change him,' continued Ketu. 'Cattlewick Cave is an ancient place of importance, from long ago in Surion times, and it is said secrets lie there. Kinga allowed him the spot permanently, and ordered the cave to be constructed to his needs. No one knows quite what he does up there. Kinga believes what he does is for the best, and that is answer enough for most dragons.'

Ketu fell silent for a while, and something stopped Yoshiko from asking more questions.

'Come now, Yoshiko,' Ketu said suddenly, veering left instead of heading in the direction of their home cave. 'Red Seventh Moon approaches. I want you to visit the Dragor Burial with me.'

It was the month when the dragons celebrated the passing of their clan ancestors. They would fly out to the deserted part of Dragor where the bones of their long-dead relations lay. Some dragons liked to rumour that the mystical Burial Ground made the spirits of the dragons rise up above it each year, and it was said that any dragon who might witness the ghosts armed with magical weapons would be rendered invincible. So every Red Seventh Moon the young hopefuls would descend on the Burial Ground to honour their ancestors, hoping to be granted the power. Each clan would bring flowers of their own colour that the Mida clan farmers had grown. During the evening, as the moon rose in the summer sky, a big colourful party was thrown to bless the dead.

Yoshiko and Ketu flew side by side, and as the wind dropped Ketu announced, 'I have something important that it is time to show you.'

The dragon clan villages grew small beneath them and the sounds of life quietened. Yoshiko flew close to his elder as they headed deep into the dragons' Burial Ground.

They landed on a barren-looking stretch of land, and Yoshiko felt an eerie energy around him. He had the strangest feeling that eyes were upon him but as he looked around could see no sight of anyone, yet he felt that they weren't alone.

Ketu saw the concern on Yoshiko's face. 'Have no fear, there are not really any ghouls around here,' he said trying to cheer him.

They sat for a moment, taking in the hush of the Burial Ground. Then Ketu spoke.

'I have been proud of you these last seasons. You look like a young warrior now because of all your efforts.'

Yoshiko looked down modestly.

'But there is something I have never told you. Something about when you were born.'

Ketu looked down guiltily as Yoshiko's face showed alarm. The elder dragon began scratching at the dusty ground where he sat, his sharp talons digging deep; he then stood suddenly and Yoshiko looked into the hole Ketu had made. Something glittered at the bottom of it.

'I see... strange-coloured shell!' Yoshiko announced hardly able to breathe.

Ketu nodded as he continued pushing away at the earth with his claws.

'It is the egg you were born from. We told the Hudrah that the whirl of colours was just the reflection of the firelight. But that wasn't true. Your egg was different, Yoshiko.

'Kiara and I took the pieces of the shell and buried them here,' said Ketu. 'We didn't want any other dragon to see them.'

Ketu reached down and pulled out a glittering fragment.

'This is where you came from,' he said. 'We tried to burn the eggshell to ash. But no matter how much fire we breathed on to it the pieces of the shell did not even get hot. They were indestructible. So we covered them in earth and left them here.'

Tears had collected in Ketu's eyes.

'We deeply wished we could keep the pieces as other elders did, in a gilded box for you to marvel at when you were growing up. But we could not for fear of others seeing it. But you need to know this, Yoshiko. Kiara and I thought your egg the most incredible thing we had ever seen.'

Yoshiko looked at the colourful pieces of shell and then back again at Ketu. He remembered Igorr's words about his strange egg.

'What does it mean?' he asked.

'I do not know exactly, Yoshiko, though I have asked the same question over and over. But something happened, before your birth. Something which made me know you would be a blessing.'

Ketu looked into Yoshiko's eyes as he prepared himself for his story. He patted Yoshiko's arm then began. 'It was back when Romao had only just won his guardship with us, and Kiara was first at her nest. Do you remember the Ageless Ones?'

Seeing Yoshiko's interest, Ketu drew himself up even

closer. 'It was a time of great worry for Kiara and me, for as soon as your egg had been laid gossip in the clans began.'

'I was in the market,' he continued, 'buying some herbs and potions, for Kiara wanted to be sure she had every medicine for the cave and would not leave the nest for fear of prying eyes. I was weighed down with cares worrying about your egg. Without thinking I sat down in front of the Ageless Ones to sort through my basket. When I looked up they were staring down at me.

'It was no different from how they usually gaze out blankly at everyone in the marketplace – but the white opal stones that they wear around their necks seemed to shine brighter – and I had a feeling, somehow, as though some kind of connection had been made.'

He looked at Yoshiko, who was staring back in silence. 'I found myself talking to them,' continued Ketu, 'of how Kiara's chest had begun to speckle before laying your egg, and of how overjoyed we were to be bringing forth a new hatchling.

'Then I told them about all the rumours and of our fears for the egg because of it being so different,' said Ketu, keeping his eyes now fixed to the dusty ground. 'I spoke of how I had to reassure Kiara of our hatchling's health when I did not feel the certainty myself, and that with many moons left to go I feared I would not have the strength to continue comforting her without more confidence. Then a strange thing happened,' he said.

'The Ageless Ones leaned forward and firmly took my arms. I gasped, having been told that the twin dragons had never been known to communicate with another dragon. I felt as though I were being pulled into another place, another time,' he continued. 'It was as if the whole of Dragor was rushing away from me and then, just as suddenly I saw myself, a few winters older, with a young dragon at my side. I knew instinctively that this was you, Yoshiko. That is when I knew that all would be well.'

Yoshiko swallowed.

'Something similar happened to me too,' he said, 'with the Ageless Ones.'

Ketu looked at him in surprise.

'When we first visited the marketplace. They stared at me and then touched their stones,' continued Yoshiko. 'I felt as though I had entered another world with them. Then came a voice that said something about destiny.'

'I do not know what to make of all this,' said Ketu.

'I know only that Kiara and I want you to be safe and happy. I thought it unfair to keep this from you now you are older.'

'Have you talked to the Ageless Ones since?' asked Yoshiko.

'Many times I have tried,' said Ketu. 'I walk past them often, but never again have they blessed me with a vision.' He stopped as if considering something, and continued, 'Without doubt, they have powers that are not known elsewhere in Dragor.'

He turned suddenly to face Yoshiko.

'But you need not worry yourself about such things,' he said as he then covered the eggshell over again with the dusty soil. 'You are now a happy and normal dragon.'

Yoshiko nodded but inside he felt a twist of pain.

He had been ready to tell Ketu about the callstone and about his visits to Guya, but now felt he couldn't. It was clear that all Ketu and Kiara wanted was for him to be like other dragons. And as time passed he wasn't sure he wanted to be.

14

The Trail Mountains

'Are you ready, Yoshiko?' asked Romao.

The day had finally arrived for Yoshiko to try out the Trail Mountains.

'I can't wait. I will be like a soaring eagle,' he said, grinning at Romao. 'I hope I can get off the first level trail really quickly and start working through to level two in a few days.'

'See how you go.' Romao smiled.

Red Seventh Moon celebrations were fast approaching and part of the festivities involved the younger dragons showing off the skills they'd now learned, and Yoshiko was looking forward to taking part.

'The first pass you'll try is quite simple,' explained Romao. 'There are no obstacles, just a few turns. The obstacles are in the harder trails and there are five levels.'

Suddenly another Guard Dragon landed by Romao. He was panting heavily.

'One of the guards has been taken ill,' he said, pausing to take a breath. 'We need you to watch over the Fire Which Must Never Go Out.'

'You need me right away?' asked Romao, instantly straightening up as he prepared to go back on guard duty.

'Yes,' said the Nephan. 'Ayo says you will be rewarded for the extra work.'

Romao unfurled his large wings.

'I have to go, Yoshiko,' he said apologetically. 'But you are ready to take on the easiest trail by yourself. You don't need me looking on. Head down towards those mountains and do some practice.'

*   *   *

As he arrived at the head of the Trail Mountains Yoshiko realised he should have asked for better directions from Romao.

Five openings lay ahead of him but there were no dragons at the entrance of any. Yoshiko was about to backtrack to the training grounds and ask which opening he should take when he heard a familiar voice.

'Well, well, well! If it isn't the hopeless Feddy!'

'What do you want now, Igorr?' Yoshiko said, turning to him.

'To see you mess up the easiest trail in the mountains.'

'Just go away, Igorr.'

'I've been flying the Trail Mountains for months and months,' continued Igorr. 'I expect this is your first time here. Perhaps you'll just about be off the baby trail by the time you're old and gnarled.'

But Igorr was looking at Yoshiko in a different way to previously. Yoshiko realised that Igorr was actually eyeing his muscular stomach and strengthened wings.

'If you want to try a really hard trail, take that one,' Igorr then said, pointing to a rocky opening. 'I fly it all the time with my elder.

'But you'll want to fly that one,' continued Igorr, pointing to another entrance. 'That's the baby trail for the likes of you.'

Yoshiko sighed and unfurled his wings. He

considered the opening to the training trail, which looked large enough.

'I will take the easy trail, I know I still have much to learn,' he said, as he drew back to take flight.

And he took to the air, heading for the training pass.

Yoshiko opened his wings out and began the steep mount upwards to swoop into the entrance from a height.

Below him Igorr started to shout something but the sound faded as he entered the training trail.

Two mountains closed either side of him, blotting out almost all the light. The gap between them was wide enough for his full wingspan, and he flapped forward, propelling himself deeper into the pass.

Up ahead the route twisted back and forth, and it was impossible to see what to expect. Yoshiko kept level, turning gracefully as the rocky sides of each mountain closed tighter and wound deeper into the trail.

Beneath him were bushes and trees, and a narrow stream following the direction of the rocks. Yoshiko wheeled in the air, feeling confident.

Then suddenly, the trail twisted sharply and the two mountains closed tight around him. Yoshiko turned quickly, narrowly avoiding grazing a wing on the rocks.

Concentrating hard, he paid close attention to the jagged edges on either side of him, expecting them to open up wider at any moment.

But as he flew onwards the trail became even more hazardous.

It was more difficult than Romao had described and the dark rocks wove ever tighter.

Several sharp turns followed, and the pass got so narrow that Yoshiko had to use all the strength in his wings to stay airborne whilst avoiding making contact.

Gritting his teeth he wound in and out of the rocks.

Up ahead, all looked black.

Yoshiko slowed, straining his eyes to see. The trail was blocked.

A web of stiff tree branches forked out at all angles, covering the pass.

Yoshiko realised with a spasm of fear that the mountain pass was too tight to turn back. The only way was onwards directly into the blockage of branches.

He tried desperately to think of a way around; he saw that the branches were blackened, and a sudden realisation occurred. It was actually a training obstacle of the pass. Dragons coming through were supposed to blow their own way through using fire.

He was already short of breath after the exhausting twists and turns, but Yoshiko drew on his reserves of energy and took a huge inhalation.

He'd have to time it just right, he considered. Blow fire too early or late and he'd crash straight into the branches and fall from the air, hitting the sharp rocks.

He saw the jagged branches come near, and let out the biggest ball of flame his belly would allow.

The fireball tunnelled through the air in front of him; crackling with heat, it blew the blacked branches flat against the mountain pass on both sides.

Yoshiko gave a great flap of his wings and shot through the gap. The trees closed back behind him, snagging his tail, and gouging into his scales. He winced at the gash that a sharp branch made.

The trail was widening again now, and an unfamiliar sight lay ahead of him.

Glowing red pools were scattered all over the ground in front of him, sending up thick plumes of smoke.

Glowing red pools.

Yoshiko peered ahead.

Lava pools.

He realised that Igorr had sent him into the most dangerous trail in Dragor. Instead of taking the training trail, he was flying the one that only the very best Guard Dragons ever managed. The shapes of the rocks were designed for one direction only and the branches had been woven layer upon layer to form a thick roof above, making it impossible to fly out. He had only one choice – to keep going.

He slowed in the air, trying to keep his reserves of energy steady.

The first lava pool approached and he turned sideways to avoid it.

A belch of hot smoke went up, scorching the edge of his wing and sending him spinning in the air.

The rapid movement was close to thrusting him straight into the next lava pool but he just managed to correct himself in time, beating his wings as fast as he could to waft the smoke down as if fanning the furnaces.

He swerved past the next lava pool, and then the next.

The fifth pool was the largest, and bubbled and spat scorching red stones into the air as it threw up one small explosion after another. Yoshiko observed that the timings between each eruption formed a regular pattern, as if it was breathing in and out.

His heart raced. If he got the timing wrong he knew the flying rocks would hit him and would probably break his wings.

As soon as one explosion finished Yoshiko decided it was time to make the biggest flap of his wings that he could. He propelled himself past the danger and with another few twists and turns the lava pools were behind him. A huge hot column of thick black smoke then shot up, narrowly avoiding his muzzle.

He was exhausted, and his wings felt ready to give out.

But a bubbling sound ahead alerted him to the fact that his trial was in no way over.

Ahead of him now were boiling hot-water springs, and the air was full of steam.

Yoshiko blinked away the hot mist. It settled on his snout in droplets. There were so many waterfalls ahead and water jets spurting in all directions through the rocks – so many he couldn't even see the end of them.

He gave a tired flap towards the hot water and just about passed through the first area, but his wings totally failed him on the second stretch where he failed to turn in time. A draft of boiling steam caught the front of wing, and he fell spiralling into a deep pool.

Yoshiko swam frantically in the red-hot water but

he knew he didn't have the strength to keep afloat for long. He felt his weight pulling him down.

Just as he was about to give up hope, he caught a glimpse of purple in the sky above.

'Yoshiko!'

It was Igorr, diving down from above.

'Over there!' he cried.

Yoshiko knew that it was his deceiver, and considered he might be trying to lure him into further danger. But he had to take the chance. It was all he had.

With one final burst of power he swam to where Igorr was signalling.

A flat ledge came into view, and Igorr beckoned him towards it.

'It is a service route in,' he called. 'The rock has been made to land on. There is a safe way out from here.'

Yoshiko flopped his stomach on to the rock as steam rose from his skin.

'You! You so nearly killed me,' he panted.

Yoshiko looked up. Igorr's purple face looked down on him, trying to look sorry.

Yoshiko spluttered and coughed.

'What sort of evil species are you?'

'I made a mistake, then I realised that if you actually

died and someone had seen me point you to that trail I would be in big trouble.'

'Mistake? Your lies will catch up with you one day, Igorr. Just get me straight out of here,' replied Yoshiko now that his energy had restored a little.

'Please don't tell on me,' said Igorr looking Yoshiko straight in the eye and trying to appear sorry.

Yoshiko paused before replying. 'Just why would I do anything to please you after everything you have done to try to harm me?'

Igorr retorted 'Well, how about if I promise not to call you Feddy any more?'

'What! You give your word! Never, ever again?' asked Yoshiko.

'Yes. I give my word. I promise I will be nice,' said Igorr nodding but hiding a wry smile.

'Then I shall give mine too,' Yoshiko agreed.

Igorr hopped up and began clambering through the service exit tunnel that opened into the mountainside. Yoshiko followed.

They reached the outside of the mountain and the rocks widened enough for a wingspan.

Igorr took off immediately, flying swiftly down to the Alana territory.

Yoshiko's scales still felt sore and his wings ached, but he had greater thoughts on his mind.

From the very top of the mountain Yoshiko could see all of Dragor beneath him. He could see far across to the charcoal tree woods where he knew the Goadah pot sat.

Yoshiko remembered the third challenge from Guya and took to the air to go to study the Goadah pot further. It was the one thing now holding him back from passing Guya's tests and discovering more.

Yoshiko arrived by a cluster of charcoal trees that hid him from view. As soon as he landed a large Guard Dragon came out of the Fire Pit.

As Yoshiko watched on, the dragon turned his back to the great clay vessel and slipped his arms backwards. The pot like magic produced two handles from its scale-like covering. The Guard Dragon bent his knees, tilted back, and lifted the pot straight up as if to exercise. As he put it down the handles disappeared.

Yoshiko gasped.

The Goadah pot. There was a trick to lifting it that had nothing really to do with strength – and the pot was truly magical.

15

Colour Control

Yoshiko kept his word to Igorr and made no mention of what had happened at the Trail Mountain. Meanwhile, he had started to train independently, although Romao often checked in on him. Day by day he felt more confident in himself.

He rose early, gathered charcoal wood and slipped into the slow heat of the Saiga Fire Pit. He loved the way that Dragor was almost empty of life as he took to the skies before dawn with only a few other dragons sharing the secret charm of the land at this hour.

He was different at Fire School too, and even his friends noticed it. Yoshiko had more self-confidence.

'You never ask for help any more,' said Amlie, as

Yoshiko carefully filled out his slab with the charcoal stick. 'You used to check with the teacher that everything you did was right. You were always scared of getting something wrong. Now you hardly ever ask.'

'I just figured it's better to just get on with things and learn by trial and error,' said Yoshiko.

Then, just a few months later something wonderful happened.

All the young dragons were talking about Red Seventh Moon. And in the atmosphere of excitement Elsy had insisted they all go back to the Fire Pit to try out their skills. Yoshiko was dreading it, knowing that the Alanas would be there, but Elsy was adamant.

'If we don't stand up to them, they'll think they own the whole Fire Pit.'

* * *

Yoshiko had felt the fear rising even before they approached the Fire Pit, and as they got closer he knew it was about to happen. He was changing colour again, and this time it was even before they had reached the pit. He knew he'd have to take flight again to avoid being noticed and began to unfurl his wings to fly off when a shout went up.

'Look! Yoshiko is turning yellow!'

Igorr had spotted the first signs of the transformation, and was shouting loudly. All the other dragons at the Fire Pit turned to stare.

Yoshiko turned to give Igorr a look of disappointment as he felt the colour rising further up through him. He reached for the callstone hidden away under his wing. It burned brightly as he held it in his claws.

The deep calm feeling he had when fanning the Effram flames came over him. He felt he was totally in control of his emotions and an inner calm filled him.

Yoshiko held on to the feeling and could sense that the gold colour was slipping back down, through his feet and away. In the next moment another shout went up.

'What d'you mean by yellow, Igorr? He's red like any other Nephan!' Igorr's friend was laughing at him.

'You're going colour blind, Igorr,' said another Alana.

The gang of young Nephans approached the Fire Pit and this time it was Yoshiko who stepped proudly to the front. He strode calmly into the outer section.

When he came out the other side all the dragons were clapping.

* * *

After that there were a few more times when Yoshiko felt a colour change rising. Once when he was in the Effram hills with Ketu. They had been looking at some incredible art and he felt a green colour spreading from his feet.

This time he responded much quicker, and after breathing deeply his scales slipped back to their normal red shade before the green even crept past his knees. Another time he had found himself frustrated in class, he looked down to see his claws were a turquoise shade like a Talana dragon. Quickly he thought back to fanning the Effram fires and it slid away.

It was as if learning to complete all the tasks had helped him find the solution to his colour changing. And Yoshiko felt ready to return to Cattlewick Cave.

16

Return to Guya

Guya was waiting outside his cave when Yoshiko arrived, as if he'd been expecting him.

'So you are back, smalling,' he said as Yoshiko landed. 'But I see actually you are not so small any more. Are you are now ready for my challenges?'

'I am ready.'

'Well, then, you had better come with me,' replied Guya.

Silently Yoshiko followed the older dragon into the enormous entrance. Today it was brightly lit as daylight with a dozen fire torches and a roaring fire in the corner. They passed rows of bookcases filled with strange symbols, and dozens of tall clay vases.

Then they walked through to the left of the cave where the walls closed around them in a maze of colourful crystal. All kinds of glittering minerals grew from the stone in pinks, greens, blues and purples.

'A smell of smoking herbs wafted out and there in the very far corner was the most complicated set of cauldrons he'd ever seen. Glass tubes, bubbling pans and pots joined a large copper centrepiece.

'That is where I make the sorrel juice,' said Guya. 'Now, are you ready to try your first challenge?'

He pointed to the Goadah pot, which had been brought inside. It was standing right in the centre of the cave.

Looking at it again, Yoshiko realised it was far bigger than the one by the Fire Pit.

Guya watched on with interest.

Yoshiko turned his back to the pot. His arms felt back for the handles and as he bent his knees they instantly sprouted out of the pot's sides for him. He grasped them and hauled the pot on to his back.

'Well done! Well done, Yoshiko,' Guya said. 'The Goadah pot chose to help you. The Goadah pot only chooses to reveal magic to those it trusts. That is the wonder of this pot, its incredible wisdom to become known only to the worthy! The other important thing to learn from it is that you have built up your physical strength by trying to lift it.'

Guya walked towards the pot and patted it appreciatively.

'Task one completed, Yoshiko,' he said as he chuckled to himself. 'Now we must come to the second task – to fly around Dragor seven times. Do you think you can do it?'

This time Yoshiko was more than sure of himself.

'I know I can,' he grinned.

* * *

Yoshiko landed back on Guya's mountain, panting but exhilarated.

'I am back,' he called. 'I have circled Dragor seven times just as you wanted.'

He walked slowly towards the cave entrance, getting his breath back.

But the older dragon was nowhere to be seen.

Yoshiko headed around the edge of the cliff, where he and Guya had first watched the lake, and made out the bulk of the older dragon. Guya was seated with his eyes closed, breathing slowly. Yoshiko approached him quietly.

'I have flown around Dragor as you asked,' he said gently.

Guya's eyes snapped open. 'Come sit here with me, Yoshiko,' he said.

Yoshiko settled himself next to Guya. 'While you have been gone I have been thinking. We have never talked of why I live alone on this mountain,' said Guya. 'I am sure you are curious.'

Yoshiko kept silent, not wanting to let on that he knew more about Guya since asking Ketu about him.

'As you know, Dragor is only one land,' continued Guya, 'the other places are not hidden like Dragor, let me show you more clearly.' Guya picked up a metal ball that was resting in his lap. 'All of the lands rest on this circle that you see. The world is actually ball-shaped. The green, brown and yellow shown on the globe is the land. The blue part is the ocean – the great waters that seem to run forever.

'They can be very peaceful,' he said, 'but then they can quickly change to storms and become dangerous. And outside of the oceans there are many battles between lands. I have a tale now to tell you.'

Yoshiko was mesmerised by Guya's words.

'A long time ago a dragon found a human in Dragor. It was a male human, and the dragon found him just at the boundaries of our great land, dying of cold. He had somehow climbed all of our defences – right over our enormous freezing mountain tops. This human was covered in fabrics from head to toe to try to keep warm and protect his sensitive skin but it was not protection enough and his body was giving up,' Guya went on. 'A dragon out in the remote mountains found him. The dragon knew that humans were the sworn enemy of dragons after they had drugged us with their herbs, trapped us with nets and held us in heavy chains. He knew that the Battle of Surion had been fought to free our kind from them, but still his heart told him that every dragon's duty is to ensure no other creature dies when it can be saved. He carried this burden, because he feared that the Council would most likely let the human die.

'And so the dragon decided that he would help the human on his own if he could. If the human lived, the dragon would try to get it back to the human world. If the human died he would take the body to the Council and admit what he had found.'

Yoshiko nodded as if listening to a fable, but he had realised that Guya was that dragon.

'The dragon took the human to a secret empty cave he knew of,' said Guya. 'There he boiled it up some sorrel juice. Slowly the dragon fed the hot juice to the human, and to his relief it drank a little. Then it opened its eyes and the dragon could see it was very frightened. The human was very small, Yoshiko, as most humans are. They are shown in pictures as larger, but in fact a human is no bigger than your leg. The human had never seen a dragon before in the same way that the dragon had never seen a human before, and it was terrified to see the huge eyes looking down on it.'

'What did it do?' asked Yoshiko.

'Well, the human was too weak to move,' said Guya.

'It soon realised that the large creature was trying to help it. So it stopped resisting and again began to drink the sorrel juice and after a while it said something. It said: "This is good."'

'It spoke?'

'Not only did it speak,' said Guya, 'but it spoke a language the dragon could understand and what was more, it spoke in the old Nephan dialect. The language that we use for formal council.'

'They speak like we do?' Yoshiko interrupted in amazement.

'It was the language of its own people,' continued Guya.

'The Nephan dialect, our dragon language, and this human's language were one and the same. Although perhaps,' he added, 'with some different words and the way we phrase things here and there, but you would be able to understand this human very well, Yoshiko, if you were to meet him. The dragon and the human became friends,' continued Guya. 'As the human got better he was very grateful to the dragon for rescuing him. He wanted to return the favour. So whilst he was recovering he tried to share what knowledge he could with the dragon. He told him the secrets of many plants which grow in deep forest areas, new herbs for sickness – those which would heal many different illnesses that Dragor had not found answers to.

'The dragon wanted to know the secrets of the human world. He told him that in his human world he was a man who liked reading books, who lived on an island. He spoke of the town where he lived having houses made of stone and discussed the things of times long ago which were buried in the earth.'

'Like what?' asked Yoshiko.

'The human world is much, much older than Dragor,' said Guya. 'Over all that time many things have become buried in the ground and forgotten. They became covered deep in the soil, and it is the job of special men to find them and dig them up without damaging them. This man was in charge of finding the bones of old animals which no longer existed. He said he was called a long name – a palaeontologist.'

'Bones of our ancestors, and dinosaurs and dragsaurs?'

Guya nodded.

'The humans only know of dinosaur bones. They know not of dragons ever really existing or indeed about the evil dragsaurs that their myths confuse with us as they haven't fully pieced together the history. This man, though – he had noticed something in his digging. He had found different kinds of bones. Ones with special teeth and signs of fire around them, where the others had nothing.'

'Dragon bones?' guessed Yoshiko.

'Yes. Dragon bones. The Battle of Surion killed many dragons,' said Guya, 'and many of their dead bodies were left around the mountains which now protect Dragor. The man noticed this. He noticed the strange bones made a ring around a set of mountains which no human had travelled into.'

'So he decided to see what was in the mountains?' asked Yoshiko.

'Yes. He climbed the mountains outside Dragor on his own looking for traces of dragons. It was an ambitious plan, for the smoke from the Fire choked him, and the cold mists froze him,' said Guya. 'If the dragon had not found him he would have died and it would have been us, the dragons, wondering what *his* bones meant.'

'So what happened to the human and the dragon?' asked Yoshiko.

'When the human was better the dragon helped him return home to his town on his home island,' said Guya. 'He flew him over the Surion Mountain, breaking the commandment of Goadah. And when he arrived in the human world he saw things of great beauty.'

Guya blinked away a tear that had formed in his eye.

'So the dragon went back to the human world often?' asked Yoshiko. 'To see his friend?'

'No. The dragon never returned to the human world. He stayed in Dragor and tried to live as he had always done, but this knowledge had changed the dragon and he became a hermit.'

'I know that dragon is you. It has to be!' Yoshiko finally announced, looking straight into Guya's mystical eyes.

'Yes Yoshiko. It is me. And I have observed you and in doing so put together many pieces of my own jigsaw,' said Guya. 'You have just circled around Dragor seven times. You have passed your second test. Now we have your final challenge. Pass this and I will tell you everything I know.'

17

Discovery

'Task three,' said Guya as they neared Cattlewick Cave. To its left was a much smaller cave. Inside it was a huge bundle of burning sticks that Guya had prepared. Yoshiko felt the searing heat of the cave as they approached. His stomach gave a little flip at the thought.

Guya led Yoshiko into the small fire cave and placed a nearby cauldron over the sticks.

'You must stay inside the cave until the sorrel juice inside bubbles,' Guya said as he exited the cave.

As the smoke closed around Yoshiko the intense heat became almost suffocating.

He gritted his teeth, willing the water to boil faster.

The sweat on his scales had become steam now, and it scalded him, rising up in a hot mist. He steadied his breathing, letting the sensation settle around him.

As the heat built it became unbearable. Every nerve in his body screamed for relief.

Everything was saying he had to quit and leave the cave. And then an inner voice spoke. *Just a little longer, Yoshiko. You can do it.*

Breathing hard he felt the heat envelop every part of his body.

And then to his relief the cauldron whistled.

Yoshiko staggered out of the fire cave, limp and exhausted, to find Guya was waiting, applauding.

'Now I know without doubt that you have a great destiny ahead!'

* * *

'Your path is not like mine,' said Guya as Yoshiko regained his breath. 'You will not dwell on an empty mountain top, though you have special gifts and this will make your life different from that of other dragons.

'The question is – are you truly ready to discover yourself?'

Yoshiko sat absorbing Guya's words. Since Yoshiko first met Guya his life had changed completely. Now that he could control his colour change he felt he could fit in with the other dragons his age. During his training with Romao he had built up enough fitness to become a Guard Dragon when he left Fire School and Kiara and Ketu would be proud of him.

But the realisation hit him that something much bigger stood ahead for him.

'I do want to discover what my destiny is.'

Guya smiled. 'I am pleased with your choice.'

The elder dragon then pressed a crystal in the wall and Yoshiko saw a complicated metal mechanism. It whirred around on cogs, revealing a secret panel that opened into a small room. Guya's flickering candle revealed some of what was on the walls.

A mixture of strange symbols and pictures filled almost every corner of the wall.

'No one knows who painted these images,' Guya said, pointing at the wall in front of them. 'This hidden cave and the images are from centuries ago, when the clans first settled here after the Battle of Surion. The symbols have been a mystery, Yoshiko. I have dedicated the last three decades to trying to understand them, but the pictures tell an easier story.'

Different dragons were painted on the walls, from various clans. Some looked as if they were fighting with one another, and others were running from little human stick figures. In the centre of it all seemed to be quite an important image, which was slightly bigger than any of the others.

'Do you recognise this dragon?' Guya asked. Yoshiko looked closely. The dragon was a Nephan shape but was made up of different colours, each colour of the seven clans. 'It's like me,' said Yoshiko suddenly. 'A Nephan who changes colour.' Guya nodded. 'I think it was foretold that you would come here, Yoshiko,' he said. 'I felt when you first came to this mountain that your arrival was important.'

'What does it all mean?' asked Yoshiko.

Yoshiko's eyes were following the images on the wall. Part of him doubted that the dragon drawn there hundreds of years ago could be him, yet something inside told him that his changing colour was linked to this destiny.

'You have waited long enough,' Guya said. 'We will now discover the truth together.'

'Look into the picture, Yoshiko,' said Guya. 'Do you see anything more?'

The painted dragon began to come to life, the colours flickered, and then it slowly opened its wings.

Yoshiko gasped out loud.

'What do you see?' asked Guya.

'The dragon,' said Yoshiko. 'It's opening its wings. It is starting to fly . . . It is definitely me! It has very large wings!' He concentrated harder and saw the big wings flapping just like his own. Then he saw himself fly high in the sky and begin circling the globe that was painted on the wall next to it.

Yoshiko said finally. 'I want to travel the skies. I need to go beyond the boundaries of Dragor,' he said. 'I can see it all, and there is something else . . .' he paused. 'I am helping the clans. I am dropping something on to them from above.'

'What are you dropping?' asked Guya.

'Something precious,' said Yoshiko. 'It is raining down on all the dragon clans.' From the animated dragon's wings, glitter fell, showering down on to the cave wall in all different colours of the rainbow.

Yoshiko rubbed his eyes shocked by what he'd just seen.

Guya pointed to another part of the wall that had been dark before. Now his candle cast it in light.

'See this picture?' he said. 'It is joined to the first. You are the first chameleon dragon ever known. You said it yourself when we met that first day. I did not know what it meant for Dragor but felt I must prepare you for something important. I always puzzled over this picture. You may think I seem strange, Yoshiko, but I am really no different from any other dragon – just with different experiences, and with my own unique purpose. It all makes sense now to me. You see, the human, he told me that the dragon bones that he found were not always buried alone. Some had gemstones buried with them.'

'What would the dragons want these stones for?' Yoshiko asked.

'The Council keep it quiet so as not to cause alarm in our land but all dragons of Dragor are losing their talents,' said Guya. 'Talana dragons are not able to dig as good caves, the Bushkis are not as good with writing and organising papers and the Nephans are not as good at breathing fire.' He waved his wings expansively. 'These and other problems were not known before the Battle of Surion. The dragon clans are all missing something, and I believe these stones hold the answer.'

'Why did we not bring the stones with us?' asked Yoshiko, thinking of the Hudrahs and their black stones, and the Ageless Ones, with the opals around their necks.

'Most stones were left in their homelands, or lost in the chaos caused by the horror of battle and bloodshed. Only a few of our stones came into Dragor. It is you who must bring them back to us. Every dragon must have his or her rightful stone,' Guya said. 'The human told me he would continue to travel the world's mountains and search for more of the stones.

'I believe you must go to him to collect the stones, to help the clans. Your wings are strong, Yoshiko, and most of all it is your colour changing that I believe will help you.' He unfurled his great wings to reveal one of them was broken. 'It was not my destiny to return.'

'And if I don't want to take such a risk?' Yoshiko asked in a small voice.

'If you decide this is not your path no one can make you follow it,' replied Guya. 'You will need to travel far. The human gave me a map that tracks both to and from where he lives. You must follow it and fly high in the sky at night and sleep away from view by day. It is a special map. It is of no use in Dragor, because what you need to see is hidden.

'Above the smoke of the Fire Which Must Never Go Out there are tiny lights in the sky at night. The humans call them stars. They will guide you.'

'I will go, Guya.' Yoshiko spoke the words with certainty. 'If I can help the clans I will go to the land of the humans and fetch the stones.'

Guya eyed him for a moment, and then nodded as if he had expected that answer.

'You must bring the stones back here safely,' he said. 'Then you must find a way to spread them into the clans. Every dragon must have his or her rightful stone,' Guya repeated.

'When should I leave?' asked Yoshiko.

'By my calculations this Red Seventh Moon' said Guya. 'That is when you must go. The stars will shine brighter on that night than they have since your birth. You must head towards the Burial Ground. When you pass the last mountain top look east.'

He took a large parchment scroll from under his wing.

'Here is the map of stars. Now that is all the help I can give you. Fail, Yoshiko, and you will never solve the problems of our land.'

18

Red Seventh Moon Escape

As the evening of Red Seventh Moon arrived Yoshiko's nerves grew. Ketu and Kiara were up early and had been preparing the food all day for the evening of festivities, and their family cave was full of red flowers to take to the Burial Ground.

It was customary on Red Seventh Moon for younger dragons to fly ahead of their elders, and Yoshiko tried to keep his shaking wings steady as he took to the skies thickened with dragon families heading the same way.

Yoshiko looked down to see torches blazing around the Burial Ground. The Council had gathered on a vast stone platform that had been assembled the previous week.

At their head was Kinga. His red scales shone in the

firelight and he was waving greetings to the hundreds of approaching dragons carrying bunch upon bunch of flowers.

Yoshiko settled towards the outer edges of the clustering dragons and turned to see Kiara and Ketu land behind him.

'Shall we have some toffee nuts?' asked Ketu, pointing with his wing towards a Bushki dragon selling the sweet nuts.

'No, thanks,' replied Yoshiko.

'All the excitement of your first Red Seventh Moon, eh? Shall we get a little closer to the Council then?' he added. 'Kinga is about to begin speaking.'

They shuffled through the crowd, and a loud noise sounded out above them.

Standing on his haunches Kinga was blowing a note through a curved golden horn.

'Welcome, dragons of Dragor!' he then announced. 'All you younglings will be thrilled as our celebrations begin in this the seventh month of our year.'

There were cheers and shouts from the younger dragons.

Suddenly a croaky voice shouted from the midst of the crowd.

'Kinga! I have something of grave importance to tell you all,' called the voice. 'Do not be so fast to celebrate!'

A ripple of shock echoed through the crowd.

'A curse has lived amongst us dragons for many years. It is time that the truth is exposed. I know that to speak of a dragon bearing a curse is at the heart of Dragor's fears, but it all must be told.'

There were gasps of horror from the crowd.

The clans began looking at each other in mistrust.

A little circle was opening up in the centre of the crowd. Yoshiko raised himself on his haunches, so he could peer at who was speaking.

It was Yula, the Nephan Hudrah.

Kinga tried to hide his shock as he took charge of the proceedings.

'What do you have to say, Yula?' he asked.

'I did wrong. I kept information hidden out of uncertainty,' she declared.

The dragons stood aside as she began to make her dramatic walk through the crowd to the centre of the Council. She reached Kinga, and bowed her head respectfully.

'Over a decade ago a dragon was born from an egg

that had been talked about throughout the whole land,' she said, her voice husky. 'Surely many of you here must remember a certain pair of elders and many rumours about a strange shell?'

Whispers started in the crowd.

'I made a dreadful mistake,' continued Yula. 'I tried to take the hatchling away before it could do harm to Dragor, but I was persuaded not to act by the father.' She pointed accusingly at Ketu. 'My instincts told me that one day Ketu and Kiara's son would bring a curse to Dragor, and as time passed I doubted my past decision not to take him in the black wicker basket. So I followed his elder and him to the Burial Ground where I finally found the evidence of his strange egg as proof to give to you.' From inside her cloak Yula pulled out a bundle of cloth, which she held aloft triumphantly.

'See here,' she said. 'I have the pieces of the shell which Kiara and Ketu have hidden from you all. Look where their youngling Yoshiko came from!'

She opened the bundle to let the shining fragments of shell fall on to the ground. As the shell dropped, the glittering colours shone, and the dragons saw them in all their glory. But the dragons nearest to the shell pieces moved away for fear of touching them. Screeches went up from the crowd as they looked at it.

'Destruction could be ahead for all of Dragor!' shouted an Alana. 'If Surion's red egg brought battles and bloodshed to dragons, then this multi-coloured shell must be worse!'

'Well, some great change is ahead, that I fear,' said Yula. 'I have more to tell because I have watched this hatchling as he has grown. I always sensed something was wrong with him and over the years I have seen him for what he is.'

She pointed an accusing finger through the dragons directly at Yoshiko. 'He changes colour!'

As all the clans turned to look towards him, Yoshiko felt the fizzing sensation through his whole body return more powerfully than ever. He fought with every part of his body as it rose furiously.

The dragons backed away from Yoshiko as though he was diseased, forming a large circle around him. A rainbow of all seven colours washed up and down his scales so quickly that Yoshiko could not control it, and then his scales began to turn purple rising from his ankles up to his waist. He closed his eyes, trying not to panic, and finally sent the colour back down through his body before he finally settled back to Nephan red.

Then there a mass of confusion, as the dragons began wondering what they had seen.

Suddenly another voice went up.

'It's true,' Gandar shouted over the dragons. 'I have seen it too. My son and I, we both know he changes colour. It happened when we were at the Nephan clan Flying Rock when he was just a hatchling. He turned Alana purple.'

'There is more,' continued Yula. 'This strange dragon often flies to Cattlewick Cave where he is forbidden. I do not know for what reason. But there can be no good in it. No dragons may go to that part of Dragor.'

This was too much for the assembled dragons, and the Alanas started shouting loudly: 'The dragon is cursed. The dragon is cursed.'

A great roar went up and everyone was suddenly silent. Kinga had blown his horn.

'Come forward, Yoshiko,' he said, gesturing to the platform.

With every nerve trembling Yoshiko made the slow walk through the dragons. Slowly he approached Kinga and as he did he felt a twinge under his wing.

He reached for the callstone that he had been hiding there and held it tightly in his claws.

YEEAAAAAA.

Suddenly the air was filled with the strangest noise.

YEEAAAAAAA.

It grew louder, and seemed to come from all around.

Yoshiko felt the noise vibrate through his whole body and a swirl of glittering white sparkles landed like snow everywhere.

The Ageless Ones appeared in front of him.

Yoshiko's jaw dropped open to see the twins outside of the marketplace.

'Heal Dragor. Delivering of the charms.'

The dragonesses spoke in harmony.

'You must complete your destiny, Yoshiko,' they said.

Yoshiko noticed that the eerie *yeeeaaa* sound had quietened all of the dragons. Charms. He turned the word around in his mind. Guya had told him about stones that he felt was his mission to return to the dragons, but what were charms?

'The charms will restore strength to the clans,' continued one of the twins. 'Dragons are not like any other creatures. They need stones found in the rocks of the earth.'

They were briefly silent as if remembering something sad, and then carried on in unison. 'Dragons of Dragor have grieved in spirit for many years. Now the time has come, Yoshiko. We have waited many years for a dragon to be able to go to the outside world,' said the dragonesses.

As they spoke Yoshiko realised that all the other dragons around him were standing absolutely motionless. They were frozen.

'We have halted time, Yoshiko,' said the Ageless Ones, as if reading his mind. 'Time now stands still, just like time has been still for both us twins. We have not aged so we could live on to help you. All so that you might return the stones.'

Their voices grew fainter.

'Even our magic was once stronger,' they continued. 'The energy has faded in the whole of Dragor and we can only halt time for a few days. It is all the time you have Yoshiko. If the dragons awaken and discover you have broken their Commandment you will be in the gravest trouble. You must hurry now.'

They bowed to him and then slowly faded from view.

'Wait!' called Yoshiko. But the twins had vanished.

19

The Land of
the Human

With his talons shaking Yoshiko took out the
parchment scroll.

'Head for the Burial Ground,' he muttered to himself,
remembering Guya's words.

Yoshiko's eyes dropped down to the map. At the
moment it was meaningless, just different dots forming
shapes and patterns that meant nothing.

He gulped nervously. Then he spread his wings and
took to the air.

Launching high into the sky, Yoshiko swooped over
the Great Waters.

Keep calm, he told himself as he remembered

Guya's advice. When you pass the last mountain top look east.

He repeated the advice.

Then another feeling swelled inside of him – the excitement of being where no other dragon had been for years.

Taking a deep breath Yoshiko wheeled and flew straight up, steeper than he had ever flown. As he gained height the realisation hit him that he was about to break one of the sacred Commandments of Goadah – NEVER FLY ABOVE SURION MOUNTAIN.

Yoshiko flew higher and higher. The smoke from the Fire Which Must Never Go Out burned at his eyes and he coughed. He grew colder and shivered beneath his scales, but his wings flapped strongly. He reached the peak of the mountain – and his heart leapt. His wings skimmed the top of the rocks as he flew up and over it.

No longer did the smoke from the Fire Which Must Never Go Out fog the air. Here the night was fresh and new. He could see a hundred lights in the sky. He held open the map and looked up. The lights matched marks on the paper, and he found he could easily follow them, and so he flew onwards. Leaning to the right he tracked the stars for a while until he began to fly over a vast ocean with the light of the full moon reflecting from it as though it could have been early dawn.

Yoshiko followed the line of water in wonder. The Great Waters in Dragor were huge. But nothing compared to this. The water stretched as far as he could see into the distance.

Suddenly the blue expanse beneath him rippled, and a huge tail splashed out of the water.

He flew lower to see more closely. It splashed out again and thumped back into the ocean, sending up a great spray all over him.

A great grey shape suddenly rose up out of the water, and Yoshiko saw that the sea creature had what looked like a single dark eye in its forehead, from which it spurted up a huge fountain of sea water that tickled his belly. He realised that it wasn't an eye at all but a blowhole – and whatever large fish it was actually had two friendly-looking eyes on either side of its head that were looking at him.

Then he remembered the whale from Ma'am Sancy's lesson – the lonely whale who had flung small fish to the Alana clan as she sought their company. This must be one of those creatures. He had met a whale!

It had sunk back down now, out of sight, and

Yoshiko scanned the waters, but the creature seemed to have vanished.

Then he felt another jet of water hit his tail as the whale surfaced again.

The whale flipped and rolled in the water, and then swam along under him, ducking down and surfacing all the while.

With it swimming beneath him, Yoshiko felt calmer about the journey ahead, and for many hours he flew with the whale alongside him.

Then, finally, on the distant horizon he saw land in sight and the whale made a bellowing noise as if it sensed something approaching. It gave a final roll in the water, and disappeared back beneath the waves.

The sky above became suddenly darker. The moon dimmed and the stars disappeared.

Guya had told him that the sky would always be full of twinkling stars, which he could use with his star map to find the stones, but now he could see nothing and had no guidance.

The air grew colder, and Yoshiko felt a wind gathering and swirling the ocean.

Then, from out of nowhere, a bolt of electricity

speared the sky, lighting up the dark clouds and the ocean beneath.

Another fork of lightning crackled over the clouds, accompanied by a booming sound, which shook Yoshiko physically.

Drops of water began to fall on his body. Within a minute rain was hammering hard over every inch of his scales like a thousand bullets. The wind swirled high around him, and with a great crash, a line of lightning came within a few feet of his muzzle as the storm closed in fully around him.

He continued on through even darker cloud while the thunder rang in his ears like deep church bells, making his head pound. Flapping his wings he flew higher, hoping to get above the clouds. Instead they grew thicker, and the lightning came in bigger flashes like fire-blasts.

Yoshiko corrected himself again and again, trying to dodge the crackles of electricity.

A huge thick bolt of power snapped towards him, zig-zagging in the sky.

Yoshiko made a complete roll, missing being struck by inches.

It's just like the lava pools in the Trail Mountains,

he thought, there must be a pattern to the way the lightning moves.

He fought on, darting and diving, responding to the warning signs that came before a lightning bolt. The clouds to his left buzzed and crackled, and a spurt of white fire shot towards him. He pulled his wings in tight to his body and let himself free-fall, with the lightning arching over his head. Up ahead another cloud buzzed and sparked, and again Yoshiko was ready for it.

He turned gracefully, allowing the lightning to snake past him, ducking and rolling to perfect timing. Then a great gust of wind buffeted him and he was thrust towards another bolt of electricity. Yoshiko dug into his reserves of strength, tipping away from it. The electricity shot past, scorching the tip of his ear, and he yelped in pain.

Just as he thought he could go no further, the rain lessened, and the sky suddenly brightened. Yoshiko saw land and a sandy cove up ahead, and flapped towards it.

He landed on the wet sand that cushioned his whole body while he caught his breath and let the soft sand run through his talons. A sudden pain in his ear reminded him of the injury from the lightning. He touched the side of his head and winced, feeling the scales on his ear that were scorched badly.

He was now desperately thirsty, and looked around for a source of water. He scanned the horizon for a stream or spring but could see nothing. At the back of the beach there was a row of tall trees that he noticed, with bright green tops and large green fruit clustered beneath.

Yoshiko stumbled gratefully towards the trees, leaning up against the trunk of the nearest and nudging down several heavy fruit with his nose.

They fell with a thud on the white sand of the beach, and Yoshiko tore off the green and brown outer husks and prised open the tough inner shells.

To his delight, they were filled with a water-like liquid. But better than any water that he had ever tasted, being slightly sweet and slightly tangy, while the insides also had a delicious sort of flesh, which he could tear out in strips.

After four of the tasty fruit Yoshiko felt refreshed. He sat for a moment looking at the white beach and assessed his options. The sun was starting to rise above the horizon. The map of the stars was of no use to him during the daytime and he had instructions from Guya that he should sleep during the day away from the sun and any humans.

He felt overwhelmed with tiredness, and made his way to a cave that lay at the back of the beach. The sound of the ocean waves lapping in the distance made his mind relax. The storm had blown far out to sea now, and the water was blue as far as his eye could see. Yoshiko let the first rays of the rising morning sun warm his scales.

Before he knew it his eyelids had begun to droop and he felt himself drifting off to sleep.

* * *

Yoshiko awoke with a sudden panic. He had slept all day, the sun was starting to set and he knew he must resume his journey.

He flew all night again, this time in still weather. On and on he went, over many lands with huge mountains like those in Dragor with their dark, vast silhouettes reflecting in the moonlight. He flew over more and more water and then hit more land. According to the map of stars he was now over the island where the human who had befriended Guya lived.

A few more hours passed and dawn was now arriving, a large cross on the scroll marked his destination. Yoshiko passed over a large river as he entered a town. Many lights shone, lighting up rows and rows of stone buildings and small streets.

He finally landed on a dusty track where he could hide himself behind some trees. Sunrise was approaching fast and Yoshiko's heart was beating loud as the thoughts ran through his mind. What if the human is not here? What if I am captured?

And yet it somehow felt as though Dragor had been a dream and this strange enchanting new land was the only reality he had known.

Yoshiko scanned the distance, looking for the house that Guya had described.

He took one final look up at the stars, sending up a little wish that they might help him.

Then he heard a voice.

'The stars are amazing, aren't they?'

Yoshiko opened and shut his mouth, not knowing what to say. The voice was just the same as the low tone of a male dragon, and very friendly. He looked around him and then he saw his first ever human.

'Are you the keeper of the stones?' The words shot out.

'Yes, I am,' the human said, smiling and laughing a little, 'and you are a youngling dragon. A Nephan if I am not mistaken. I know this of course from your red colour.'

'I am Yoshiko of the Nephan clan,' said Yoshiko formally. 'I have come to find the keeper of the stones.'

'Well, Yoshiko,' said the human. 'Find me you have. You may call me the keeper of the stones if you wish, but I would prefer that you called me Gopal. That is how I am known to my friends in this country.'

Yoshiko felt a rush of relief. 'Guya told me I should find you here.' But he couldn't help himself from staring at Gopal's strange shape.

'Come. Follow me. Guya told me a dragon would come to me one day.'

'How did you know I would come tonight?'

'The same way that Guya must have known to send you,' said Gopal. 'Come quickly before people wake and see you.'

Gopal began to walk down a pebbly drive. Yoshiko went slowly after him, glad of the chance to stare at the retreating figure that moved on two long limbs, which hardly looked like they could hold him up. Then there was the matter of the human's scales. They were so fine that they were invisible to the eye and he looked fragile as if the slightest talon scratch would cut deeply. Gopal had cloths, as Guya described, fitted over most of his scales. On his head was a patch of thin greying fur, which Yoshiko assumed had grown to keep his head warm.

'Is this your cave . . . errr, I mean what Guya said is called a house?' asked Yoshiko with hesitancy.

The human laughed again.

'It is my equivalent of cave, my house, yes.'

He beckoned Yoshiko to follow.

'Guya taught me much,' added Gopal, 'but I have learned even more from my many travels. I have been to the homeland of each and every dragon clan after Guya explained them to me.'

'Guya told me that you know about stones in different colours. The same colours as our dragon clans,' Yoshiko said.

Gopal nodded. 'Stones. Yes. Since meeting Guya I have been collecting the stones.'

They passed an extremely large door to the side of the house. It had been made especially tall and wide, and Yoshiko could see that another wooden building had been extended from the bricks at the back into the garden. At the very top were glass windows allowing the sunlight to shine through.

As they approached Yoshiko had a calming feeling.

It was as if all of his nerves were melting away, and the nearer to the hut they came the more relaxed he felt.

Gopal took out a large key and fitted it into a padlock that held shut a large gated entrance. It turned easily.

The gate opened and light flooded out.

Yoshiko gasped.

The wooden building was hung with thousands of glittering stones.

Once they were inside Gopal lit a candle, and the incredible colours spilled forth even brighter.

Every shade of the rainbow was represented, and Yoshiko felt his eyes grow wide as he saw them.

'I call the building the House of Halos,' Gopal sighed. 'I have always felt as if I am surrounded by great forces, like the crowns of angels when I am in here. My hobby is to craft things, out of metalwork or anything I can get my hands on that inspires me, and I feel the energy here feeds my creation.' Gopal reached up and pulled down a red stone. 'The dragons of old times loved these precious stones that you see. They treasured them.' He passed the deep red stone to Yoshiko, who took it slowly.

Warmth seemed to pulse from it.

Gopal let out a long breath as if wondering how to explain. Then he sat down and gestured for Yoshiko to do likewise.

'Most people in the lands outside of Dragor do not believe in magic,' he began. 'They live their lives chasing money. It is what they think is the most valuable thing. During the great battle between the humans and the dragons so much was lost. It pains my heart to even think about it.'

Gopal continued, 'I have travelled through my life and seen the caves where all the dragon clans first lived across the world far and wide. In the back of the dragon caves their stones formed naturally from the minerals of the rocks.' Gopal pointed upwards to further illustrate the array of coloured stones.

'The earth is old, and holds deep within her great power. And each of your clans needs the stones of its homeland to have their own full power.'

Yoshiko gazed up at the hanging stones, taking in the truth of Guya's words.

173

'Can't we just go back to our original mountains?' asked Yoshiko. Gopal shook his head.

'These places became ruled by humans even before the Battle of Surion. The dragons were kicked out of their caves, captured and made slaves, and most humans would fear dragons too much to let them return if they met them again. But there is a solution,' he said.

'What is that?' asked Yoshiko.

'Taking stones to the dragons,' said Gopal. 'What you are here to do.'

'If I bring stones to the clans will all the problems be over?'

'There will be problems in Dragor whilst the clans disagree with one another,' Gopal said. 'At the moment there is nothing you can do about that, but the stones I believe will help restore the dragons' talents at least. The dragons will regain their true powers and feel healthier in their bodies. And I hope no humans will ever find you! No humans or indeed dragsaurs.'

'Dragsaurs?' Yoshiko asked, horrified, thinking about the stories of the grey beasts without souls that once pillaged the clans and murdered the dragons without a thought. 'Why do you mention dragsaurs? They are long since extinct!'

'Yes, that is thought to be correct and in the name of Surion let's hope it is,' Gopal answered. 'But with what I have witnessed in my life, nothing would surprise me. My instinct just tells me that Dragor absolutely must restore its strength for things to come. For its own happiness at least – hoping it will never need it for any other reason than that . . . Now then,' he added, 'let's get moving. You need to be going. There are seven different stones here for you. The Nephans can now have the ruby stone from their homelands. This is what you are feeling when you're here, the peace of being so near the stone of your lands,' he said as he handed Yoshiko a red gem. 'That is your rightful stone.'

'It seems to give me energy and a feeling of confidence,' he said.

'Good. That is how it should be,' said Gopal. He gestured towards another array of stones, deep blue in colour. 'These are sapphires,' he explained. 'This dark blue stone helps the dragons make better medicines. These are amazonites,' he went on, moving now to a pile of light blue stones. 'They give strength.'

Gopal thought for a moment. 'Only I no longer call them stones,' he added. 'I have attached something to them. It is what allows them to hang from the ceiling here.'

Yoshiko looked closer at the red stone in his hand. It was attached to a little metal hook.

'It makes them more than just a stone,' said Gopal. 'They have been fashioned as a decoration for the dragons. So that they can wear them around their necks or arms and keep them with them at all times.'

'So what are they now called?' asked Yoshiko.

Gopal smiled. 'In the human world we would call them charms,' he said.

Charms. Yoshiko remembered the words of the Ageless Ones. *Heal Dragor. Delivering of the charms.*

'What are these?' asked Yoshiko, pointing to the array of green and deep yellow jewels.

'Those are the green jade and the yellow quartz,' said Gopal. 'The first enhances creativity. It could help your Efframs make more incredible pots,' he added. 'And this quartz is great for vision, it will help with the failing eyesight of your Bushki clan.' Gopal was then pointing to the last charms that were orange and dark purple. Yoshiko thought carefully.

'Well, the Midas are not as good at growing crops

as they once were,' he said, pointing to the orange charms first.

Gopal nodded. 'True. Those are sunstones, and will renew their farming spirit.' He was standing by the purple charms. 'These are amethysts. This helps dragons breathe better so they can fish and dive under water for longer. I must confess I am not sure how you will scatter them,' he said with uncertainty. 'But my job with them is done. Now, Yoshiko. You will need to rebuild all your strength for your return. Sit and eat with me. I made a fish stew for you. I remembered Guya's recipe that he once showed me. '

Yoshiko followed Gopal into the house, just squeezing through the huge door that had been specially made. A large rug was in the centre of the living room. Yoshiko had to crouch down on it, but was comfortable eating and chatting there with Gopal as though they were longtime friends. Gopal told him about his friends, three children who lived locally in his town and often visited him. He talked about the games the children would play in the town, just like Yoshiko and his friends would do in Dragor. He then shared a famous ancient story, about a famous castle in the south-west coast of his island where a king called Arthur and a magician once lived with dragons. He also told him many tales about a famous writer called William who once lived in his town, how this famous man wrote about love and the wars between the rulers of the different human lands, and how even today young men throughout the world had sacrificed their lives in wars – a very brave soldier he knew had lost his. Yoshiko began to get a clearer picture of human nature and felt great sadness that the world could not be united. Yoshiko ate all he could, Gopal stoked the roaring fire and the dragon slept for the whole day.

Evening had come again and Gopal woke Yoshiko. 'Time for your journey home,' the old man said as Yoshiko opened his big green eyes. Gopal took one of the red charms, threaded it with a piece of string and hung it around Yoshiko's neck. 'For extra energy! It will make the journey home so much easier.'

He then loaded the charms into seven bags and flung them into a large net over Yoshiko's shoulder.

They waved to each other as Yoshiko headed back into the night.

'Take care, Yoshiko,' said Gopal. 'I know you will deliver the charms.' Then he waved with both arms as Yoshiko launched into the sky, leaving the house of the human far behind him.

20

The Gift of Charms

Yoshiko began following the map in the reverse direction, heading back towards the smoky skies of Dragor. The journey home seemed much quicker despite the weight of the stones. As he flew by darkness and rested by daylight his mind was entertained recalling the many stories Gopal had shared with him.

Dawn was breaking once more and his homeland came into view. Yoshiko headed for the top of Surion Mountain hoping that from there he might know what to do. He landed on its peak and took the seven bags of stones out of the net. He laid the charms in front of him in seven neat piles. At that exact moment there was a loud thump, thump, either side of him. He turned to see the twin dragons had landed in front of him.

Looking down at the charms with the twins at his side something occurred to Yoshiko. His mind flashed back to the visit to the Herb Doctor when he observed the odd scales on his wings, the ones like hooks that the doctor had offered to clip away.

Curiously he unfurled his left wing and leaned around to look underneath.

The Ageless Ones spoke together. 'You were born,' they said, 'to drop these charms. You must make a different trip for each colour, clipping them to your scales. Seven trips, for the seven clans.'

Yoshiko thought back to his training with Guya and how he had worked up his strength to fly as quickly as he could around Dragor seven times.

'There is not much time left, Yoshiko. The dragons are beginning to awaken, for we have halted time for as long we can,' said the Ageless Ones. 'We have used our powers to help you further – all dragons of Dragor have had their memories wiped about your birth eggshell and your colour changes. It is as if the declaration about you by Yula to the Council never happened. But, Yoshiko, we can halt time no more!

You must deliver the green stones, and when you have finished come back here and we will give you the next colour.'

'I will be as quick as I can,' said Yoshiko, looking up to Dragor's dark sky as the Ageless Ones helped hook the charms to his scales.

Launching back into the night sky Yoshiko headed into the smoky skies of Dragor. As he flew the stones around his body moved in a happy sound, like bells. It was a soothing noise and he let it ring into the night sky with the charms sparkling.

He wondered how he could drop them correctly.

Then suddenly Yoshiko could feel a familiar sensation, a colour change was happening and by the light of the moon he could see that he was turning a bright green. He realised he must be above the Effram clan.

Yoshiko fluttered his wings very quickly and the stones fell from his scales, down over the Effram terrain.

The first charms were gone, and Yoshiko wheeled in the sky, heading back to the mountain top.

The twins were waiting for him, and started to load on to him the next batch – the orange charms of the Mida clan.

Yoshiko repeated the process for all the clans, and

then finally delivered the charms of his own clan, the red rubies.

* * *

That day was one the dragons would talk about for years to come. Unaware that they had been frozen in time for days, the dragons awoke to discover the blanket of coloured gems had fallen like a rainbow before them, giving each of them a special feeling. They each took a charm and tied it around their necks and used the rest to decorate their caves.

21

Fire Games

As Yoshiko neared his family cave entrance he saw the Council Spear resting outside.

He knew that the spear meant that Kinga was inside with his elders. Letting his talons scrape the rock as he landed he braved himself, hoping that they too held no account of Red Seventh Moon .

Inside he heard the voices of Ketu, Kiara and Kinga.

He thought back to Yula's speech to Kinga at the Burial Ground where she labelled him Dragor's curse. But the voices sounded happy.

His first sight of the dragons was of them sitting drinking sorrel juice and smiling contentedly.

Kinga was the first to see Yoshiko.

'I have just come to share some news with your father, Yoshiko,' he said, greeting him normally.

Ketu came forward to the mouth of the cave holding a ruby-red stone.

'Do you feel it?' Ketu said, holding the stone close to Yoshiko. 'All the dragons have had them delivered from the skies!'

Yoshiko smiled, not knowing what to say as he touched the red ruby charm Gopal had given him.

Kiara had a blissful smile on her face. The line of worry, which Yoshiko often saw marking her brow, was gone completely. 'It is a miracle,' she said, and then Ketu spoke. 'Yes, some miracle has come to the clans from the skies, bringing gifts for us all.'

'We shall celebrate with a carnival and competitions tomorrow in honour of this blessing, I expect to see you take part in the Fire Games,' said Kinga to Yoshiko.

'I'll happily enter the Fire Pit event,' replied Yoshiko, smiling to himself.

A few seconds later and a great fanfare echoed.

'It is the Guard Dragon,' said Kinga. 'I must go now and make a speech.'

Kinga bowed to Kiara and Ketu.

'I look forward to celebrating with you and all the other clans,' he said. Then he took off high into the sky.

* * *

That evening Yoshiko and his elders joined the hundreds of other dragons from all over Dragor who had been summoned. The whole land sparkled from the jewels that they had all hung around their necks and none showed any signs of recalling the Hudrah's dramatic outburst.

The Council had assembled again on their grand platform.

Once all the dragons of Dragor were present, Kinga spoke.

'A great blessing has just fallen upon Dragor,' he said. 'Charms fell from the sky.'

'They sought out the different colours of the clans. All of those who feel the special power of these charms raise your claws.'

All talons were raised aloft in agreement.

'We must be sure to give thanks for this gift,' said Kinga. 'We must also discover if there is another part to the puzzle. If any dragon knows of how these charms came to be delivered, speak up and we will hear it.'

There was silence amongst the dragons.

'Then it is a gift from Goadah himself,' said Kinga.

But Yoshiko could have sworn that Kinga looked straight at him.

* * *

It was the most glorious carnival that Dragor had ever known, filled with colour and cheer. Every type of fire breathing and sporting event took place, as well as many other talent competitions to show off the dragon's skills in their magnificence.

The Mida dragons had competitions for the best flower arrangements and the Efframs for the most uniquely crafted pots. The Alanas competed for who could catch the largest fish and the Bushkis for the most cleverly scripted poetry. The clans all excelled and it was clear that their talents had been restored to their fullest glory.

Late in the afternoon The Great Races began. Yoshiko watched on with great pride as Romao achieved the fastest time through the most difficult Trail Mountains and was awarded a special medal. Then as dusk approached came the last of the Fire Games – the Fire Pit Challenge.

* * *

Yoshiko stood at the entrance of the Fire Pit, and Igorr stood beside him as a fellow contestant. A youngling from every clan had been selected to take on the Fire Pit challenge with Amlie and Elsy representing their clans and Cindina watching over her friends with nervous anticipation. Ayo and the Fire Guards had been heaping up fuel and blowing huge bellows of air into the flames to heat it. All other dragons lined up. Ayo blew a silver horn and all the younglings began to venture forward into the flames, one slow step at a time. Whilst the other dragons were already sweating and guarding their eyes Yoshiko was finding it easy. He moved quickly into the outer pit, and up to the line which divided it from the centre. He then waited a few moments as other younglings approached. Igorr was the first to draw up alongside him.

'Enjoying the heat, Yoshiko?' he said.

'I sure am. It's hardly hot at all,' Yoshiko replied, and on a sudden whim he stepped into the deepest part of the pit.

Suddenly a vicious-sounding voice yelled, 'Go on, Igorr!' It was Gandar, shouting at his son. 'Don't let the Nephan beat you! Go after him. Show him what you're worth.'

Igorr's face turned suddenly angry and instead of taking a step deeper into the pit his thin snout twisted in pain and he walked straight out to face his elder squarely.

'If you want to win an award for our family, then go enter a competition yourself,' he retorted. 'But then again you only do things you can cheat at,' he added bitterly.

Gandar's mouth dropped open in surprise.

The whole crowd had silenced for a moment to listen to Igorr and Gandar.

Yoshiko had felt a burst of satisfaction as Igorr fell back. Amlie had by now ventured far beyond other dragons her age and beyond Igorr. She received applause as she departed the fire and ensured she gave both Igorr and Gandar the biggest smile that she could.

Inside the pit, Elsy was next to Yoshiko, side by side the friends stood, having beaten all the other dragons. Elsy now shouted against the noise of the flames: 'Go, Yoshiko, you can do it. Go get the Flaming Spear.' And he made his retreat.

Yoshiko ventured on into the heart of the fire and grabbed the Flaming Spear.

The crowd were on their feet clapping as he returned triumphant and he allowed the heat to fall from his scales as his friends screamed in delight. 'Our hero!' cried Amlie.

The noise of his audience continued almost deafening, and it was Ayo who greeted him first.

'No youngling your age has ever been able to endure that heat,' he announced. 'You are the winner, Yoshiko. As your reward for such an achievement you will now train with my elite – to be a warrior of Dragor. And you shall be granted the future honour of guarding the Fire Which Must Never Go Out.'

Yoshiko stood proudly as he could see Ketu waving in the crowd and tears of joy rolling down Kiara's face.

'Time to say some words,' Ayo said. 'The platform is yours.'

Yoshiko walked up the steps and stood looking over all the crowds.

'Fellow dragons!' he announced. 'It is my proudest moment to have acquired the Flaming Spear!'

The words seemed to be tumbling forth as the dragons made more cheer.

'We dragons who live amongst the rocks have stones

returned to us which have magical powers. We must use them for greater good. The future is ours to decide.'

*　　*　　*

A feast was then held with huge bowls of the freshest fruits, and sticky mash, followed by limestone pies and honey cakes. It was all washed down with enormous cauldrons of sorrel juice. There were fire displays from the various clans, and a group of Guard Dragons flew across the Great Waters with flaming torches in a special performance of their skills.

*　　*　　*

As Yoshiko celebrated in the marketplace he remembered Guya. He didn't like to imagine his friend alone when all the other dragons were feasting, but as he looked across he could see that Guya was out of his cave, waving happily at him in the distance.

*　　*　　*